KILLING ZONE

"Go!" He heard Slater's voice in his ear as the Shan United troops finally came into position.

At this notification of imminent meltdown, Bishop opened up with the Commando on burstfire mode and with the sound suppressor unthreaded.

The disoriented force of soldiers, hearing the sound of ratcheting burstfire and seeing muzzle flash in the distance where there had been none before, immediately rushed pell-mell toward the source of the gunfire without thinking that they were being led into a trap.

Soon the force was in the killtrap. Waiting a few beats, Slater triggered the phased claymores.

In a matter of seconds the violent spasm of destruction unleashed by the claymores and the autofire had taken out the entire force of Shan United infantry pursuers.

Also available in this series:

FORCE OPTION

DAN MATTHEWS

SLAM

White Powder, Black Death

A GOLD EAGLE BOOK FROM
WORLDWIDE®

TORONTO • NEW YORK • LONDON
AMSTERDAM • PARIS • SYDNEY • HAMBURG
STOCKHOLM • ATHENS • TOKYO • MILAN
MADRID • WARSAW • BUDAPEST • AUCKLAND

First edition August 1993

ISBN 0-373-63408-0

Special thanks and acknowledgment to
David Alexander for his contribution to this work.

WHITE POWDER, BLACK DEATH

"As policy becomes more ambitious and vigorous, so will war, and this may reach the point where war attains its absolute form."
—Karl von Clausewitz

PROLOGUE

In the backseat of the air-conditioned car that sped along the modern six-lane highway, Victor Chin could feel his pulse thunder in his ears. After years of hard work, he had almost reached the end of the line.

The Audi was bringing him to a face-to-face near Mae Sai, Thailand, with Kuhn Sa, the drug warlord who controlled the largest guerrilla army in the Golden Triangle.

From the Shan Mountain poppy fields cultivated by the hill tribesmen under Kuhn Sa's control came sufficient quantities of raw opium base to supply the world's demand for heroin two times over.

Kuhn Sa was the first link in a long chain that stretched from the drug producers and refineries of the Shan, down into Thailand and ultimately into the needle-scarred arms of junkies across the United States.

Victor Chin glanced at the man sitting beside him on the backseat of the luxury sedan and then at the one beside the driver.

Both members of the drug syndicate, or triad, were recruited from Chiu Chow, a region of China that was to the Chinese what Sicily was to the Italians: a breeding ground for killers.

If either man suspected even for a moment that Chin was not a Chinese-American heroin honcho ready to close a multimillion-dollar deal with Kuhn Sa, Chin knew that they would snuff out his life with less remorse than most people felt about swatting a fly.

If they knew that Chin was a Drug Enforcement Administration undercover operative who had been placed inside the New York White Crane tong some two years before with the precise objective of setting Kuhn Sa up for a fall, then Chin's death would be as slow as it would be brutal.

But they suspected nothing. Victor had made sure of that. He had been recruited precisely because he was unknown to the drug world.

Born in Vietnam, Chin had joined the U.S. MACV/SOG program at the age of sixteen.

The SOG crews had placed Vietnamese civilians beside American Special Forces irregulars, Aussie commandos and French Foreign Legionnaires for covert assignments. After the war Chin had gotten his citizenship papers and enrolled at UCLA, but given his testing ground in life, felt sorely out of place in college.

His search for some meaningful cause to devote his life to had led him to the DEA. His military experience, national origin and native intelligence had made Chin a very attractive recruit. More than that—Victor Chin was the answer to a prayer.

The DEA had unsuccessfully been trying for years to penetrate the Chinese triads, which were named for the triangle symbolizing the forces of heaven, earth and man. They had all but given up the mission as undoable, the war as unwinnable.

Established in China hundreds of years ago, the triads seemed impenetrable. The organization spread to the New World, but no outsiders were accepted, and only native Chinese were normally admitted.

Yet the triads wielded immense power. Using the tongs, Chinese protective and fraternal societies, as front organizations in the U.S., they engaged in drug trafficking, white slavery and vice.

Because they were linked with the criminal triads operating out of Hong Kong and Thailand, the tongs had the backing of an international organization doing a yearly business equal to the gross national products of most Third World countries.

In only a short time, Victor Chin had achieved what had never been accomplished before. He had been accepted by the White Crane tong in New York's Chinatown.

Chin had risen quickly in the organization's hierarchy. So great was the trust he had gained from the tong's elders that he was now being used as an intermediary on one of the biggest heroin deals ever done by the White Crane tong.

The deal would firmly establish the tong as the single largest supplier of heroin not only in the United States but also in Canada, Mexico and South America.

The horse was triple-nine-grade China White. It was of a grade purer than any yet imported to America.

Aside from the destruction in human life that the flood of heroin would unleash, the untold millions that the White Crane tong would amass from the deal would spark a war between it and rival tongs to consolidate White Crane's control.

The fighting would certainly claim hundreds of lives, if not more, by the time it was finally over.

Yes, thought Chin to himself as the modern highway gave way to a primitive jungle road and the Audi suddenly lost speed. They would kill him like a fly. They would have no other recourse.

Suddenly the man beside Chin became animated.

"We have almost arrived," he said, showing tobacco-stained teeth as he smiled. The butt of the 9 mm semiauto holstered beneath his jacket was exposed as he raised his arm and pointed ahead of them, into the jungle-covered distance.

FROM THE LANDING PAD of the villa at Mae Sai—a veritable fortress owned by one of Kuhn Sa's generals named Yuen Tat Chow—a Bell helicopter lofted Chin across miles of jungle impassable by any other motorized means of transportation.

From a border town adjoining the Golden Triangle at the junction of Burma, Laos and Thailand, the chopper quickly shuttled Chin into the heart of Kuhn Sa's realm and the headquarters of his private paramilitary force, the Shan United Army.

After twenty minutes' flying time, the Bell chopper set Chin down in the middle of a dust-choked landing zone cleared from the triple-canopy rain forest. Thatch-roofed huts and bamboo longhouses, all supported on stilts against flooding in monsoon season, surrounded the primitive LZ.

From his aerial vantage point, Chin could see military vehicles of various types parked nearby. This was no army in name only, thought Chin to himself. Kuhn Sa had enough firepower to fight a small border war, if need be.

There was more than just hardware, though. Far more. Chin saw that clearly, too. This was the terrifying part.

Seemingly thousands of the general's troops thronged the area, all clad in olive drab jungle BDUs and porting various derivatives of AK rifles—from the short-barreled AKR "Krinovs" to the standard AK-47 assault weapons. It was a vast sea of men, each fanatically loyal to the person of Kuhn Sa, whom they worshiped as a virtual god.

A man in fatigues met Chin as he exited the chopper. He introduced himself as Dao Lin, the drug warlord's right-hand man.

After shaking hands with Victor Chin, Dao ushered him toward a large tin-roofed hut through a corridor formed by the parting sea of the Kuhn Sa's guerrilla soldiers.

Chin knew that the show of force was being put on to both intimidate and impress him. By demonstrating his enormous strength, Kuhn Sa would assure his guest that he was not to be trifled with, letting him know that a deal once struck was a deal already done.

"Ah, Mr. Chin," the warlord of the Shan said, coming out of the hut to meet Chin and warmly embracing him. "I am pleased to meet you. The honorable men of White Crane tong have spoken very highly of you."

"As they have of you," Chin told Kuhn Sa. "Of you they say, 'he is one on whom heaven bestows blessings, and men bestow respect.'"

"I am unworthy of such high praise," Kuhn Sa said with a small laugh. "But come inside. There are others I would like to introduce you to."

Within the hut's cool, dark interior, Chin met the "others" Kuhn Sa had mentioned.

"Mr. Yip and Mr. Lao have also been eager to meet you."

Suddenly Chin felt the blood in his veins turn to ice water.

He had been burned. One look at them told him that.

"Glad to meet you, sir," the one called Yip told Chin. "We greatly look forward to doing business."

Suddenly Chin felt himself grabbed from behind. The hand gripping his suddenly pushed his arm aside, feeling beneath his lightweight tropical suit jacket for his semiautomatic weapon and quickly pulling it from his holster.

The two Chiu Chow who had accompanied Chin to the villa and arrived at the base camp separately by Range Rover threw Chin into a chair and bound his wrists. Chin could not suppress the cold sweat that poured down his face.

Mr. Yip smiled. Following his eyes, Chin saw why.

His partner, Mr. Lao, was holding a syringe and filling it from an ampoule of clear fluid, tapping the side of the hypo as he slowly and carefully retracted the plunger.

One of the Chiu Chow flicked open a stiletto and cut a slit down the sleeve of his jacket, baring Chin's right arm, then tied a plastic hose around it to expose a vein.

Mr. Lao bent close.

"Yes, we look forward to talking to you, Mr. Chin," he said, plunging the tip of the hypo into Chin's vein and depressing the plunger hard.

PART ONE:

Slam the Hammer

The safehouse was situated on an elm-lined George-town street in Washington, D.C.

Turning the corner and walking to the middle of the block, Deal Slater hung a right and climbed the short flight of weathered granite stairs to the freshly painted door, noting that the armored security camera mounted overhead was already recording his presence to unseen surveillance personnel within.

He entered a small vestibule and walked up the flight of hardwood stairs with a walnut balustrade to the room on the first floor of the Federalist-era town house.

Already there ahead of him were Mason Hawke and Eddie Bishop, the other two members of the three-man covert strike unit known as SLAM. The acronym by which the team was known stood for the search-locate-annihilate missions that were its specialty, and each part of the acronym defined specialist capabilities.

Search—covert and high tech. The unit had priority clearance for Intelsat transmission from remote positions worldwide.

Locate—mission parameters encompassed infiltration of criminal organizations by unit personnel in order to elicit Intelligence critical to the success of the planned military option.

Annihilate—the team had broad weapons-requisitioning privileges with no restrictions on cost or provenance. Special atomic demolition munitions, SADMs, could be requisitioned by presidential order for tactical nuclear strikes against priority targets.

Missions—mete out punishment to the criminals at the heart of interlocking global drug conspiracies with dire consequences for the United States and its allies. The strike team was only deployed as a course of last resort to destroy criminal enterprises by armed force, when all other means had been exhausted.

Along with the two covert field operatives, Jack Callixto, SLAM's liaison with its Intelligence support activity within the National Security Council, known as Yellow Light, was present.

Jack Callixto's usually relaxed face was tightened into a grim mask. Since he had the aquiline nose and high cheekbones of the Indian stock of southern Mexico from which he was descended, he could look formidable when angered. He recognized Slater's presence with a restrained nod. Callixto's low spirits were shared by both Hawke and Bishop, who uttered only perfunctory greetings.

Noting that they were seated in the comfortable leather club chairs placed along one wall of the opulently decorated town house, and that they faced a large-screen digital television, Slater seated himself alongside his two men.

"I don't have to make any speeches about the importance of this mission," began Callixto now that the team was assembled in the briefing room. "Especially to you, Deal. So I'll just give you your brief."

Callixto was right: the mission's vital nature was an article of faith to Slater.

Victor Chin and Deal Slater went back a long way together, back to the fusion cells in Desert Storm and even before that, all the way to Grenada and the final months of the war in Southeast Asia. Slater had been present at Chin's wedding and was the godfather to his son.

Callixto hit the Play button on the VCR remote. The CIA seal appeared on the screen, the head of a bald eagle surmounting a shield containing a compass rose, and above it the slogan, And Ye Shall Know The Truth And The Truth Shall Make You Free, along with a warning noting that what was to follow was UMBRA coded, to be viewed only by those bearing the highest security clearance.

As Slater watched, it occurred to him that logos had infiltrated virtually every aspect of contemporary life.

Desert Storm might not have had as much TV coverage as Nam, but it had the distinction of being the first war with its own highly stylized 3-D logos.

In keeping with the aesthetics of an age of designer wars, Slater supposed he'd have to get used to Intelligence assessments on videotape bearing flashy logos, too.

The image of the photo-reconnaissance Intel was grainy but of reasonably high grade. Slater recognized it as an oblique-angle shot, the kind normally gathered by high-flying reconnaissance aircraft such as the TR-1, probably sent out from Tak Lee in Thailand.

The data fields on the upper left and right of the screen identified the site as Mae Sai, Thailand, a northern border town not far from the city of Chiang Mai. The time was 0700 hours.

The successive frames showed the mansion belonging to the heroin lord General Yuen Tat Chow. The main building was surrounded by a high perimeter wall. There were barrack buildings for the small army of retainers guarding Yuen by day and by night.

After several images flashed on the screen, Callixto freeze-framed the VCR and used a laser pointer to indicate a portion of the main building.

"We think Chin's in there. We're fairly certain that he's still alive, but how much longer is anybody's guess. The CIA's operations directorate has worked up a plan, gentlemen."

Callixto outlined the plan to Slater, Hawke and Bishop.

The three commandos listened and assessed its strengths, already "war-gaming" it in their minds to test it for weaknesses and the unrealistic expectations commonly found in plans worked up by men on the Langley building's seventh floor.

In the present case the plan appeared reasonably sound on its face, and after Slater, Hawke and Bishop added some suggestions, the strike team made a final decision: the mission would be a go.

Jack Callixto confirmed the new plan and was already crafting the wording of the report to the brass in such a format as would not lead to its being further watered down or committeed to death.

As SLAM's liaison with government, that was part of his job, and it was a job that Callixto performed well.

SLAM's members left the safehouse individually. The men would not meet or speak with one another until the team had been inserted into the strike zone, some twenty hours from that point.

2

The cell was little more than a box made out of cinder blocks and a poured concrete floor. Its windows were heavily barred and casemented with the far end not wide enough for an adult to squeeze through even if the one-inch-diameter iron bars were cut through.

From the casement window, Victor Chin could look out onto the compound enclosed by the security walls of the estate belonging to General Yuen Tat Chow.

He tugged at the bars although he knew that the effort was futile. Escape seemed virtually impossible, and Chin's actions were more of a tension-releasing mechanism than a true test of the bars' capacity to resist his strength.

Although Chin knew that he could not have been at his place of confinement for more than a few days, he was having trouble keeping track of the passage of time.

This mental process was the outcome of captivity in environments that deprived the human senses of regular input. The human mind began to deteriorate rapidly after only a brief time under such conditions.

The door opened unexpectedly, startling Chin with the sound as it banged inward against the cinderblock wall of the cell.

"Out!" the guard barked in Hakka, the Chinese dialect of the region, gesturing with his short-barreled AK in case there was any misunderstanding of his meaning on the prisoner's part.

Victor Chin was taken from his cell and brought into another room. He was beaten with bamboo sticks and forced to stare into a videotape camera for long minutes.

Chin guessed that the footage would be used as proof of his continued existence. Such proof might be needed by his jailers to show to anyone interested in his release. After this session he was brought outside into the compound.

Chin knew why this was happening, too.

It had happened to him once before during his stay as the druglord's "guest." General Yuen Tat Chow knew the orbits of the KH-11 satellite assigned to this area, and thus knew when it was due to pass overhead.

From its 150,000-foot-high vantage point in polar orbit, the KH-11 photo-reconnaissance satellite could resolve objects as small as eight inches. It was easily accurate enough to ascertain that Chin was still alive and reasonably well.

After the passage of a few minutes, during which Chin faced his AK-toting guards, the ferret-faced head guard issued further orders in Chinese. Waiting on his commands, his men sprang into action, dragging Chin back to his cell and leaving him to his increasingly unendurable solitude.

SLAM's COMMAND POST in Bangkok was established in a warehouse owned by an international holding company that in reality served as a front organization for the Central Intelligence Agency.

It was one of many such CIA "proprietaries" held throughout the world and designed to fulfill various operational roles from weapons caches to operational planning centers and even to covert prison facilities.

In the present case, the top floor of the two-story warehouse had been outfitted as an operational command center and situations room. High-speed modems with DES standard encryption-decryption hardware linked the facility to NSA computers via military communications satellite.

Weapons storage and repair facilities, as well as physical training areas, had also been established on the covert site.

The CIA's asset on the ground in Bangkok was a Vietnamese-American named Tony Lee. Like Victor Chin, Lee had begun his career as a covert Intelligence asset at a young age, acting as a scout for Phoenix Project teams in the final years of the war in Southeast Asia. From there he had been assigned to Hong Kong and later to Thailand.

Expecting the SLAM team's arrival, Lee had already conducted a preliminary probe of the target site that the mission had been crafted to take down.

Earlier that morning he had made visual contact with Victor Chin, who had been brought out into the protected compound to be identified by the orbiting KH-11 Intelsat in high earth orbit.

On his soft probe of the target site, Lee had taken a Zeiss-Nikon automatic camera loaded with an ultrafast film and equipped with a high-resolution telephoto zoom lens. He had snapped off two rolls of film and had developed these into a series of glossy black-and-white prints.

These shots of SLAM's operational strike zone now festooned the illuminated face of a large light board in the center of the situation room.

Slater, Hawke and Bishop were seated in chairs taken from computer work stations in the operational area. They looked on as Lee ran the SLAM strike team through the latest Intelligence he had gathered on his secret run.

Lee described the terrain features in detail, traffic in and out of the estate and other pertinent factors. Slater found Lee's narrative more focused than the CIA videotape viewed by the SLAM team during Callixto's mission briefing in Washington and the Intelligence relayed by him fresher still.

Asking a series of perceptive questions based on thoughts and concerns raised by the late-breaking Intel, the SLAM crew was able to fine-tune the dominant strategy that underlined their mission plan to a far greater extent than had been possible before their arrival in Thailand.

In addition to late-breaking Intel on the strike, Lee was also sitting on the weapons and gear that would be deployed on the rescue strike.

The gear was in a series of hardened transshipment modules. The SLAM personnel immediately broke out the matériel and inspected it, checking the items carefully against the equipment manifest provided by the on-site computer.

Everything appeared to have been delivered as ordered, the packages bearing the now-familiar barcoding strips of the military's quartermaster corps.

Three SITES Spectre submachine guns were among the first of the weapons inspected by the SLAM crew. The Italian-made 9 mm SMGs were of an advanced design and specially threaded to take the Sionic-type silencers with which the team was equipped. In addition to their formidable 50-round magazine capacity, the subguns incorporated a special toroidal firing system for greater accuracy.

But perhaps their most innovative feature was that the Spectres were full double-action weapons. They fired from a closed bolt, much like a conventional automatic pistol, and didn't have to be cocked before the first round could be discharged.

Advanced AN/PRC 3000 comsets were another important element of specialized gear that the strike team would take with them into the mission zone.

The lightweight comsets worked well on tryout, their central processing units fitted into pouches on milspec load-bearing suspenders, and their headsets, incorporating a miniaturized earbud and ricegrain microphone, were comfortable to wear and compatible with the Litton AN/PVS Gen-III NVGs—night-vision goggles.

But operation of the LTID, laser targetillumination device, also included in the manifest, would be the responsibility of Mason Hawke alone as the SLAM team proceeded on its rescue mission.

As the strike team's technical officer, Hawke's expertise would be indispensable in this critical mission element despite the fact that it would mean his participation in the strike would be relegated to a supporting role. Although his presence would be missed by Slater and Bishop, Hawke was to play a role that was of critical importance to the success of the rescue plan.

In fact, part of Lee's purpose in carrying out a recon of General Yuen Tat Chow's estate had been to select the high ground necessary to deploy the LTID while Slater and his men were inside, taking care of their end of the mission.

This Lee had done and done well.

He had selected a primary and a backup site in the event that the primary could not be reached due to unforeseen operational contingencies. He was a little afraid of what would happen, though. He had heard about the LTID and the destruction it was capable of unleashing.

One thing was certain: it would be something to remember.

3

At 0434 hours, the SLAM team deployed into the central focus area of strike operations.

All were now in full battle dress: milspec jungle BDUs made of pure cotton ripstop material with four-pocket shirt and six-pocket pants. Lace-up jump boots incorporated tempered steel shanks, firm web supports and vulcanized rubber soles.

Load-bearing suspenders were slung with HE, Frag and APERS minigrenades while SIG-Sauer P-228 personal sidearms rode NATO-standard UM-84 universal military holsters in quick-draw tanker configurations. Magazine pouches containing reloads studded the nylon webbing, too.

The CPUs of the rescue team's AN/PRC comsets were also carried on the suspenders, snug and stable in easily reachable radio pouches equipped with constrictor straps. The Spectre SMGs were ready but locked, the automatic weapons safed for the immediate present.

Tony Lee drove the team toward their jump-off point. This was situated less than a kilometer from the heavily fortified border estate where the subject of the operation was being detained by Yuen Tat Chow.

Turning off the main highway, Lee steered the four-wheel-drive vehicle across rugged back roads for several minutes until he reached the spot he had located on his previous tactical recon conducted on the day before.

"Here's where you guys get off," he told his passengers in the back of the van. "*Swasdi,* as they say in these parts."

"Thanks, and *swasdi ka,*" Slater told Lee as he and the other two members of the covert rescue team exited the vehicle. "We'll see you back here no later than 0600 hours. If we're not back, don't wait around."

"I know the drill, Slater," Lee responded, sounding a little peeved. "And I can follow procedures as well as anyone else." As support infrastructure, he felt sensitive to being patronized by field personnel, even though he knew he shouldn't.

Lee sat in the van and watched the three shadow warriors disappear into the dense jungle underbrush. A few moments later they had vanished from sight like the mythical *phi bop,* or spirits, said by the locals to inhabit the jungles and bring misfortune to the wicked and unjust.

AT APPROXIMATELY the same time as Slater and his strike crew were exiting the van in Thailand, another mission element was going into action some four thousand kilometers to the northwest at Riyadh, Saudia Arabia.

At an airstrip established for strikes into Iraq during the air phase of the Desert Storm campaign, a black-hulled aircraft of advanced design was taxiing for takeoff.

Called "the Roach" or "the Wobbly Goblin" by the majority of its pilots who were not given to romanticizing the machines as much as those who watched them perform from the sidelines, the aircraft had already become the stuff of myth.

Arranging permission for the flight from the Saudis had involved no small amount of diplomatic maneuvering. It was a process that, but for the rapport gained during the Gulf War, might have been impossible to bring to fruition under any other circumstances.

The permission, once given by the rulers of the desert region, had cleared the use of the advanced aircraft in support of the ground mission in Thailand.

The F117A had distinguished itself by a one hundred percent survivability rate during its night bombing missions over Iraq, and in a very short time from its takeoff, the Stealth fighter would again distinguish itself in support of a covert mission. The principal difference now was that no acknowledgment of its role could ever be officially made.

Inside the internal weapons bay of the Stealth was a modified BLU-82 "Daisy Cutter." The multithousand-pound air-to-ground munition—first developed to carve out landing strips in Vietnam—was essentially a "dumb" iron bomb outfitted with a Paveway guidance package.

The Paveway upgrade kit would allow the F117A to deliver its bomb load with the unerring accuracy made famous in reports from the gulf.

Paveway's canarded seeker head would lock on to infrared laser radiation and be routed to the target, all the while transmitting television images to the F117A's battle-management recorder.

The pilot was one of the veterans of the gulf's multimission operational environment. He knew little about the mission he was tasked with tonight, but he did know enough not to ask too many questions, just to strap the plane to his back and do what the Air Force paid him to do.

Since he had volunteered for the job, the pilot figured that with his decision to undertake the mission came the responsibility of following the need-to-know rules of the spooks for whom he flew the aircraft.

For the present there was nothing for the pilot to do except allow the F117A to fly him to his destination, and this function the Stealth fighter performed exceedingly well, with the benefit of air-to-air refueling tanker support.

The aircraft was on autopilot mode and flew its "black line"—the course vector drawn on the plane's mission chart—with unerring accuracy directly to its target.

Taking advantage of the Stealth's adjustable padded cockpit seat, the pilot sank below the level of the cockpit window and turned up the gain on his Walkabout, feeding more volume to his earphones. The CD was by Guns 'n' Roses, one of his favorite rock bands, and he wanted to enjoy the ride until it was time to take over.

PUSHING ASIDE the black nylon tactical cover of his chronometer crystal, Deal Slater noted that they had reached their stopping point, code-named Royal, according to schedule.

The SLAM team was now situated on the strike zone perimeter, a shallow rise above the compound affording a reasonably direct line of sight toward the main building of the estate.

Through night vision goggles, each member of the three-man commando unit scanned the central area of operations below them.

Slater could discern the primary target clearly against the green viewfield of his NVGs, which utilized third-generation light-amplification tubes of an effective antibloom design.

As he scanned the strike zone, he reached up and used the brightness-control reticle to adjust image quality. Due to the brightness of the stars as the team emerged from the cover of the jungle, the image was a little too intense.

From his scan he determined that activity levels at the base appeared normal. There was no suggestion of a heightened level of alertness that might indicate expectations of a covert attack.

Slater judged that operational factors warranted proceeding with the mission. At Slater's hand signal acknowledgment, Mason Hawke removed the heavy rucksack hoisted on his back and unslung the precision combat gear he had brought along.

As the technology expert of the team, deployment of the LTID was his responsibility. Unfortunately this meant that Hawke would remain at Royal while Slater and Bishop deployed to their second recon point, Kingpin.

Hawke was already setting up the LTID and calibrating its sight as his two partners moved out.

4

Halting at Kingpin, Deal Slater and Eddie Bishop conducted a final recon of the strike perimeter prior to moving in and attempting to take down the target.

A scan of the area through NVGs assured them both that the tactical situation remained stable and that their positions weren't compromised by unfriendlies.

Slater glanced at Bishop and nodded. Both men unsafed their Spectres and felt the familiar surge of adrenaline that occurred immediately prior to engagement in armed combat, sparking the primal energy of man's fight-or-flight reaction.

Reaching up to grasp the talk button stud on the AN/PRC comset nestled in its radio pouch on his load-bearing vest, Slater depressed the button twice to produce a double click.

AT HIS STATION at point Royal, Mason Hawke heard the double click in his compatible unit's earbud and he knew that Slater had just sent him the go order.

Hawke sent his own double acknowledgment clicks and experienced the immediate calm he felt whenever a mission had reached the stage of commitment.

From that point on his gut told him that there was no turning back and he could go about his work with a feeling of complete focusing that translated into a razor-sharp mental clarity unlike anything else he had felt at any other time.

Hawke was still engaged in calibrating the LTID, confident that the other two members of SLAM would be deploying into the strike zone.

VICTOR CHIN DRIFTED in a troubled state somewhere between sleep and wakefulness.

In the darkness of his prison cell, he opened his eyes and stared up at the ceiling, seeing the jerkily moving shadows that were cast by palm fronds disturbed by the gentle overland night breeze.

For a few fleeting moments he had believed himself to be somewhere else, in the Los Angeles apartment where he had made his home. But the awareness of his true situation returned all too quickly, and though Chin wished that he could again lose himself completely in its embrace of sweet forgetfulness, he knew better than to believe that he could willfully reenter the narcoticlike dream state.

Not moving, he lay awake in the darkness, listening to the sounds from within and without as he watched the shadow play on the ceiling.

Against the faint rustling of tropical leaves, he heard the barking of a dog from far off and the faint yet constant hum that pervaded the silence, a mechanical hum that seemed to emanate from deep within the building and that he couldn't identify.

Fully awake now, Chin continued to listen and watch as he lay immobile on the hard cot. Apart from the sounds he had detected, the wing of the building in which his cell was located was utterly silent.

Yet Chin knew that the silence was deceptive.

Outside in the corridor that ran past his cell, General Yuen's guards would be on patrol. These armed men weren't truly soldiers; they had more balls than skill, more aggressiveness than brains, yet the AKR Krinov autorifles they ported made them a presence to be reckoned with.

After a while he heard the rhythmic sound of faint footfalls in the distance approach from the corridor outside and grow louder as they came nearer to his cell.

Keeping his eyes tightly slitted, Chin watched the door for any sign of activity. Soon he saw the judas hole set in its face slide to one side and an eye belonging to one of the guards peer in at him.

Apparently satisfied that the prisoner in his charge was asleep, the guard shut the judas hole again with a sharp rasp and continued to walk his post.

In a few moments his footsteps receded entirely, and Chin's cell was silent once again, save for the rustling of the palm fronds and the barking of the dog who, like himself, was awake in the middle of the night.

WHAT THE PRISONER couldn't hear, and what he had no way of knowing, was that silent shadows were converging on the position—night-stalking warriors whose mission was to break him out of his cell.

Deal Slater and Eddie Bishop crouched just beyond the perimeter visible to the low-light TV cameras that slowly swiveled on their iron pintles as they panned across the bare apron of ground stretching beyond the security wall of the compound.

Slater waited until the precise moment when both of these security cameras were tracking in such a way that a temporary blind spot was fleetingly created between them. He signaled Bishop to move into position.

Sprinting across the few feet separating their position from the wall, Bishop had his back to the wall and his silenced autoweapon tracking back and forth as Slater waited until the cameras again circuited on their orbits.

When the window for action was again open, Slater joined Bishop at the wall. They unshipped their climbing gear and soon Slater was scrambling up the length of milspec nylon rope while Bishop stood guard below.

At Slater's signal to proceed, Bishop also scaled the wall, and in moments the climbing rope was again stowed away in its gear pouch riding Slater's load-bearing suspenders.

Both SLAM commandos were now on the other side of the security wall that ringed General Yuen's estate. Slater and Bishop crouched and scanned the compound. A moment later they were already in motion, and events had passed the point of no return.

5

The guard walking his perimeter didn't catch sight of the shadow that was edging up abreast of him.

In the split instant when he realized that he was targeted for termination by the dark man-shape at the edge of his peripheral vision, it was already too late for him to help himself.

The sentinel pivoted, and there was fear and shock etched on his face as he brought up the short-barreled Krinov in a sharp, sudden motion.

The reflexive response did the sentry no good.

Slater was already pointing the blunt nose of the silenced Spectre SMG at the head of the target earmarked for disposal.

From a distance of less than three meters, there was no way he could miss. A trigger squeeze from a finger protruding from a black tactical-gloved hand unleashed a 3-round burst of Hydra-Shok ammunition.

The Hydra-Shok rounds, like the better-known Glasers, had been designed to produce an explosive effect on impact, resulting in high terminal ballistic energy transfer.

Unlike Glasers, which release hundreds of tiny pellets on impact, the Hydra-Shoks utilize both pre-fragmented hollownoses and a central metal cylinder to achieve a similar destructive effect.

As the rounds impacted on the left dorsal process of the guard's skull, fragments of the prescored bullet razored through cranial bone and brain matter, simultaneous with the expansion of the now-semimolten metal rod that had both mushroomed and deformed.

The combination of these factors resulted in the destruction of over thirty percent of the sentry's cranial mass, and he sagged to the cold earth with a large, blood-disgorging exit wound in his skull.

Almost simultaneous with Slater's takedown of the first sentry, Bishop had acted to silently terminate a second guard.

Within seconds both victims of whispering death were being dragged to places of concealment, leaving an unguarded sector of the compound across which they could proceed toward the main building about one hundred meters from their present position.

Their Spectres ported at the hip and still set on 3-round burst, Slater and Bishop loped across the safe corridor they had cut out on low-profile crouches.

In minutes they had negotiated the compound to stop short of their primary site of ingress, which had been selected from a careful analysis of aerial surveillance photos.

This site was a locked metal access door at the rear of the service area of the building. From the surveillance photos it couldn't be determined with certainty if the lock on the door could be picked or if it would need to be blown.

While the two-man crew designated Team Zircon carried specially muffled button charges for this purpose, they would only be deployed as a fallback option.

Mason Hawke, SLAM's expert on locks, had studied the surveillance photos and considered the job doable.

Hawke had been able to identify the lock type with a fair degree of certainty as a rim cylinder device. During the team's stay at the mission support facility in Bangkok, he had drilled Bishop in the technique of using a modified torque hammer to pull the cylinder.

Bishop had mastered the technique to quickly and effectively neutralize that type of lock, but this was the field and Bishop was well aware that any number of complications might arise.

This time around, anyway, the technique did indeed perform as effectively as Hawke had claimed it would.

While Slater covered them both with the Spectre in his gloved fists, Bishop used a torque hammer to pull the cylinder with a minimum of effort and noise. Moments later Team Zircon was inside the target structure.

At once the tactical situation changed, bringing advantages and disadvantages in its wake.

No longer did the two commandos require their NVGs, so they stowed them in their gear pouches. But in the lighted corridor beyond the compromised steel door, they were also exposed and their ability to take cover was severely compromised.

Slater and Bishop encountered no threats as they loped toward the corridor's end, weapons tracking from left to right as Bishop scanned their rear flank for unfriendlies. At the far end of the passageway through which they moved was a T-shaped branch with a stairway to the right.

This stairway, both men knew, led down to the basement level of the building, where Chin was being kept on ice. Both were also aware of the fact that their luck was bound to change and they were highly alert for the presence of guards as they took the stairs with Bishop in the lead.

The pace of action accelerated almost immediately.

Three guards were in the area just beyond the stairway. Slater and Bishop took them down with pulsed bursts of fire and dashed past the anteroom into a short corridor beyond.

Here another sentry in paramilitary field dress came rushing toward them but he caught a burst from Slater's sound-suppressed SMG as he struggled to point his rifle. He went down quickly, the noise of his body thudding to the deck making more of a racket than the bullets that had killed him.

Slater and Bishop proceeded silently down the now-deserted corridor and reached the section containing the row of prison cells. While Bishop stood guard at the entrance, Slater checked the judas holes one by one.

He spotted Chin on his second try.

ARMED with a spare Spectre, Chin joined Slater and Bishop in a fast sprint through the corridor.

Stepping over the bodies of the terminated sentries, they proceeded in reverse using a leapfrog strategy. While Slater and Chin moved forward through the corridor, Bishop covered them until they had again reached the exterior of the doorway.

At the door Slater again consulted his wrist chronometer. They were a few minutes ahead of schedule, he noted.

So far, the operation had been executed without a hitch. Luck, skill and speed had all combined to bring Team Zircon to its mission objective, and now they were on a downhill slope.

But extraction carried its own dangers. If they didn't successfully extract from the compound within fifteen minutes, they could count on meeting a singularly unpleasant end.

It would be an end that had nothing to do with the opposition and everything to do with the mission that Mason Hawke was now carrying out on his lonely hilltop some distance away.

There wasn't a spare set of NVGs for Chin, but he wouldn't need the goggles if the operation proceeded as planned. And if it hit a snag, there might not be much any of them could do.

Donning their NVGs, Slater and Bishop moved abreast of Chin toward the extraction point, where they would ascend the wall and hopefully come full circle to the successful conclusion of the mission.

Halfway to their objective, the team realized they would never make it as blazing klieg lights came on and sirens began to wail, rending the night asunder.

6

Mason Hawke took another look into the reticle of the LTID's bore sight.

Although its emission was invisible to the unaided human eye, the unit's sensors continued to report strong readings as the device beamed its lance line at the side of the estate building.

Suddenly, from his position crouched in the spider hole he had dug for concealment and protection, Hawke saw the muzzle-flashes of automatic-weapons fire.

These were originating from the compound below him. With the flashes came the bright red streaks made by tracer rounds, and Hawke heard the alarm sirens and the shouting of frightened and enraged men.

His view of the developing situation was partially obscured by the estate's concrete perimeter fence, so he couldn't clearly make out what was going on. But Hawke didn't need to know any more than he already did.

The operation had hit an unforeseen glitch: Slater, Bishop and the man they had risked their lives to rescue from the druglord's prison were apparently all in a world of hurt.

Hawke's jaw tensed as he strained to discern any additional clues to what was happening below. Located at position Royal, call sign Diamond, he was under strict orders to maintain radio silence, as were Team Zircon and Lee, who was at his station, code-named Emerald. However, with the fire zone now hot, those orders no longer were in force.

"Zircon, this is Diamond," Hawke spoke into the rice-grain mike of his AN/PRC commo headset. "Say your situation."

AT THAT MOMENT Slater and Bishop were standing back-to-back with Chin in between them as they traded fire with General Yuen's retainers.

The fast-cycling fire of the Spectres was countered by the duller, slower and deeper reports of the AKs and short-barreled Krinovs ported by the opposition as 7.62 mm rounds drilled their way into the dirt at either side of their boots.

"We're taking fire!" Slater shouted into his own mike above the growing din of battle. "Do not intervene," he continued. "Hold your position."

"I copy that," Hawke said. "You've got eleven minutes to get clear."

"Affirmative," Slater said back. He knew damned well that every tick of the clock brought them closer to death. "Carry on at Royal. RV at Emerald."

"That's affirm again, good buddy," Hawke said back.

As Hawke got his gear ready, anticipating the destruction that would take place within minutes, Slater spotted a way out of what would otherwise be a zero-sum game.

An armored four-by was parked only a short distance away. Slater shouted for Chin and Bishop to head for the vehicle while he covered their tracks.

Suddenly he took a hit in the shoulder, and blood started to spurt immediately; his action had exposed him as a lightning rod for hostile fire.

But by this time Bishop was already hot-wiring the ignition while Chin wielded a chattering, flame-belching Spectre SMG in one hand and Bishop's SIG semiauto in the other.

The ignition turned over just as Slater dodged inside the war wagon, hearing the thunking of the heavy-caliber slugs as they hammered in a hail against the armored hull of the vehicle.

"Go!" Slater yelled as he fired through one of the gun ports in the vehicle, then reloaded while Chin, crouching on the other side, continued to fire steel-jacketed PBs at the opposition.

Bishop, who knew the stakes as well as Slater did, needed no further incentive to floorboard the gas pedal and catapult the war wagon forward at a high rate of acceleration.

He thanked the general for his choice of wheels as 7.62 mm rounds impacted against the steel-hard bulletproof glass of the windshield when he barreled the car through the striped barricade at the main gate.

Although tire-slashing traps sprang up that were capable of ripping any conventional tires to shreds, the armored car had self-sealing gel-filled inner tubes and wasn't hindered as Bishop wrenched the wheel to bring it onto the main road.

SIXTY THOUSAND FEET above their heads and about seventy miles to the northeast, the F117A reached the epicenter of its strike envelope.

The pilot, who had long since removed his Walkabout earbuds and put his CD player away in a personal gear pouch, now scanned the ground-mapping screen to one side of the control panel.

The color raster of his FLIR—forward-looking infrared—tactical display showed that he was in position over target. In a few moments the pinging tone in the cockpit advised him that his laser designator had acquired a lock on a source of radiant energy from the ground.

From that point on, computerized targeting systems took over the show. The pilot's role would be to choose between the options of abort and continue.

As the FLIR scope showed a target lock, the pilot chose to continue the mission. He depressed the button on his joystick and pickled off the bomb load.

From the belly of the Stealth, the multithousand-pound-high-explosive bomb tumbled like a huge black stone torn loose from the dome of heaven. The Daisy Cutter's tail stabilizers quickly placed it in a nose-down position as it fell below the look angle of the fighter plane's nose-mounted FLIR sensor, and DLIR—downward-looking infrared—took over to put the pickle in the basket.

The bomb had been used against the Iraqis in the Gulf War, and it was the most destructive nonnuclear munition ever produced. Its destructive power could shake the earth and produce a firestorm on impact. Augmented with the Paveway seeker head, the BLU-82 was highly accurate, able to strike targets with unmatched precision.

The pilot's attention was now focused on the phototelemetry screen, which was flashing him a real-time display of the imagery as seen from the Paveway seeker head.

Framed in a white box reticle while altitude and azimuth data flashed at the margins, the structure illuminated by the laser beam on the ground was clearly visible.

It grew larger and larger as the aerial munition neared it. A few moments later the image blanked out, and the pilot could see the bright flash of the detonating warhead many thousands of feet below.

Having confirmed the strike, the pilot proceeded to execute the remainder of his assigned orders.

Performing a wingover, he set a course heading back to base, whereupon he would turn over the videocassette record of the strike for Intelligence analysis and grab himself a cold brew and a hot shower.

ALTHOUGH MASON HAWKE was well away from the blast zone and knew full well what to expect, the reality of what he witnessed was almost impossible to believe.

From the epicenter of the blast, in what had only a heartbeat ago been the extensive compound of General Yuen's mansion, there now was a burgeoning pillar of fire.

The mushroom cloud, made up of thousands of tons of pulverized rubble, earth and rock, rose up into the sky, terminating in an incandescent balloon. As Hawke hustled from his site, taking the LTID with him, he felt the earth tremble fiercely underfoot.

Hawke reached the site of Emerald minutes later. Lee had his weapon trained on him when he arrived. The CIA ground asset's eyes were wide, and his face wore an awed look.

"Sweet Jesus!" he exclaimed. "You nuked it!"

"Negative," Hawke replied. "That was a conventional munition. A big one, granted, but conventional just the same. Any sign of Slater and Bishop?"

"Nothing," Lee replied, shaking his head. "I heard shooting before the blast."

"That was them," Hawke replied with a nod. "They were taking fire."

Silently they looked at each other. They knew what their orders were: get out of the area as quickly as possible. Still they waited, Hawke knowing in his gut that Slater, Bishop and Chin had made it out alive.

"We've got to go," Lee said after tense minutes had passed.

"You go," Hawke told him.

"We have orders!" Lee replied. "You can't just—"

But Hawke had silenced Lee with a suddenly raised hand. Now Lee could hear it, too: the roaring of a powerful automotive engine nearing their position.

As they took cover at either side of the armored vehicle, bringing their weapons to bear on the direction from which the sound was coming, each of them prayed that it was Slater.

The sudden appearance of the black armored car almost drew their fire. It certainly would have if not for Slater's voice in the earbud of Hawke's comset.

"Couldn't raise you before," Slater said as he stepped from the vehicle, Bishop hustling Chin in front of Slater. "That BLU blast played merry hell with the local atmospheric conditions."

"Good to see you, guy," Hawke said.

"Good to be here," Slater returned. "That goes for all of us."

Lee hit the gas pedal and roared the van out of the wait position, heading through the early-morning darkness toward an isolated landing strip on the outskirts of Chiang Mai. From there, Chin and his rescuers would be flown to safety by a CIA-chartered twin-engine Beechcraft Baron.

7

High and green, their flanks dotted with fertile vegetation and the valleys between them watered by drenching seasonal rains, the Shan Mountains are the primary source of the world's opium supply.

It has been estimated that over ninety percent of the world's heroin comes directly from poppies grown in the Golden Triangle region. When converted into raw opium base, the yield of this crop makes its way along ancient mountain trails that wind their way toward transshipment and processing sites on the coast.

From that point on, the flow of heroin is shunted into a variety of drug pipelines, most of which terminate in the United States of America, the drug's principal consumer.

While in recent years the epidemic of hard narcotic use has spread to Europe, America still ranks as the primary marketplace for the drug that begins its deadly journey in the Shan Mountains.

The Shan region is a dangerous place, a danger belied by the primeval beauty of the almost virgin countryside. The production of the opium fields is overseen by warlords whose private armies are frequently equipped with the latest in military matériel, and they rule the region with fists mailed in iron and wills to match.

The warlords of the Shan aren't indigenous. In fact, they are strangers in a strange land. They are the remnants of the forces of Chiang Kai Shek, which fled mainland China in the years following the Chinese Communist revolution.

During the Vietnam era, it is said that these ousted generals from the Chinese mainland struck an unholy bargain with U.S. Intelligence services. In return for acting as a buffer against communism from the north and south, they were allowed to grow and sell opium and to purchase arms with the proceeds of these illicit transactions.

The most prominent of these heroin warlords was a man calling himself Kuhn Sa, although that was not his real name nor was much known about his origins.

The only fact of real significance was that Kuhn Sa commanded what was by far the largest army in the region. Well trained and highly motivated, his Shan United Army was fanatically loyal to its warlord, who had successfully withstood all attempts aimed at bringing an end to his dominion over the drug trade.

USUALLY, the mind of Kuhn Sa was as clear and untroubled as a high mountain lake. But on the morning following the destruction of the estate of the chief vassal of his sprawling drug fiefdom, Kuhn Sa for the first time in many years found himself confronted by a premonition of impending disaster.

At first he hadn't been able to believe what his ground assets were telling him.

It was in itself unthinkable that a small force—it was said that only two men comprised it—succeeded in breaking the captive DEA agent from General Yuen's heavily fortified compound.

But the reports that Yuen's estate had been completely destroyed by a hellish explosion that completely leveled everything within a quarter-mile radius and scorched the earth to a vitrified crust—that was truly beyond belief!

Yet the photographs that he had been shown didn't lie. They demonstrated beyond all possibility of fraud that the damage was as extensive as Kuhn Sa had been told.

The scope of destruction was unimaginable.

What sort of munition had been used to produce such carnage? he wondered. By what method of delivery had it been made to strike its target? Finally, who had ordered this strike, a strike of such devastating magnitude that it rivaled anything he had ever witnessed in his long military career?

The answers to Kuhn Sa's first two questions were as yet unclear. Perhaps they might never be completely known to him. But the answer to his final question was obvious.

The Americans were responsible.

Only they had the technology to inflict damage on such a gargantuan scale with seemingly undetectable weaponry.

And in this knowledge of the obvious grew the bitter seeds of revenge, Kuhn Sa knew as he conducted his t'ai chi exercises in the mist of a balmy mountain morning. The American giant had flexed its muscle, seeking to inflict death on what it regarded as little more than a troublesome gnat.

But had it not acted in very much the same manner almost two decades before? And had it not failed utterly in its mission because of the brilliant tactics of Ho Chi Minh?

The answer to both these questions was yes. Kuhn Sa would employ similar tactics in his retaliation.

Already he had gathered preliminary Intelligence on the location of the operatives who had carried out the strike. They would be taught a lesson, Kuhn Sa pledged.

Once again, as had happened times before, the American giant would be stung by the gnat it had sought to swat.

AT THE CIA's national photographic interpretation center located in the agency's headquarters building at Langley, Virginia, Intelligence analysts were already at work on interpreting the data brought back following the Stealth fighter's clandestine night strike in the skies over Thailand.

Prior to analysis, the flight videocassette data had been digitally enhanced by computer equipment rated at an ultrahigh-speed sampling throughput. Although the results were expected to be extremely high-grade, they astonished even the veteran analysts who believed they had seen it all.

They had watched as the television imagery from the Paveway's seeker head showed the BLU-82 descending, then striking the target with perfect precision. Slow-motion replay of the moment of the blast demonstrated that this accuracy was matched by destruction on a level exceeded only by a hit by a nuclear device.

However, the most spectacular imagery from the strike came not from the Paveway video footage but from real-time telemetry collected from two other sources.

These were a KH-11 satellite in polar orbit high above the site of the blast and a Lacrosse radar imaging platform circling in geosynchronous earth orbit.

Both these orbiting eyes in the sky showed the genesis of a firestorm caused by a single conventional bomb strike.

The munition's initial detonation flash was followed by the roaring pillar of fire and a plume of black smoke that rose hundreds of miles into the stratosphere before being caught by the jet stream and blown northeast.

In the aftermath of the blast, destruction was complete.

The charred hulks of vehicles were caught in the surrounding jungle, where secondary fires still burned. Ground zero itself was little more than a ten-meter-deep bomb crater, encircled by a fringe of earth fused to glass by the furnacelike heat produced by the strike.

But from the standpoint of the analysts, the best news was that the damage had been well contained.

The strike had been sanitary.

Because of the location of the target far from major urban centers and arterial highways, collateral damage was negligible. This factor alone meant that the Agency had been able to deliver on its promise to the President.

There would be no heat-blistered faces of innocents to prick the conscience of the world. There would be no villagers forced to leave their land and take shelter in refugee camps.

The voices raised in protest of the strike could be easily silenced. The storm would blow over.

The Agency had fulfilled its mandate to the President. From this mission the CinC would have what presidents cherished most from their Intelligence services: plausible deniability.

8

Slater left the modern high-rise hotel where he had been registered as a sales representative for an American tool-and-die manufacturing firm under the flash ID supplied by Jack Callixto prior to the mission.

Upon his return to Washington, the passport identifying him as "John Avery" would be returned and recycled for use with another legend for yet another agent in the field of covert operations.

Hailing a taxi from the stand near the hotel, Slater gave the driver directions to Bangkok's Don Muang International Airport. Slater was anxious to return to the States and to be debriefed.

And though Thailand boasted certain hedonistic pleasures that lured many American travelers to it, including opium dens and willing *bon tok* girls of *sanuk* houses, these were not for Slater. For him, Thailand would always be associated with Vietnam and the unpleasant memories of the final years of the war in which he'd served with MACV/SOG.

About the only thing Slater would miss about Thailand was its superb cuisine, which to his mind was better than any other fare found in all the Far East.

Fatigue had set in as Slater yawned and leaned his head back on the seat cushion. But fatigue was as dangerous to the mind as it was to the body.

Because he was tired, Deal Slater had failed to take more than passing notice of the van pulling away from the curb as the taxi left the curb by the hotel.

Had he been more alert, Slater might have noticed that the van maintained its place several car lengths behind the taxi as it negotiated the streets of downtown Bangkok on its way toward the highway leading to the airport.

But there was no possible way that Slater could have known that inside the van, solidly bolted to its floor, was a MAG 7.62 mm machine gun. Its pintle mount allowed it a full one-hundred-eighty degree field of fire through the aperture formed when the side doors were rolled back.

Nor could Slater have known that besides the machine gunner and the driver of the van there were three other men on board the vehicle, or that each of them was armed with full-auto firepower and gunning for him.

HAWKE AND BISHOP were already at the airport, booked on a nonstop flight to Dulles International Airport outside Washington, D.C.

The two SLAM commandos were awaiting their flight's embarkation announcement in a bar just outside the airport's departure lounge.

The local beers served by the smiling Thais were excellent, and they lingered for a while before getting up and leaving for the departure lounge to get their seating assignments and await the announcement of their row numbers.

Behind them in the crowded terminal, a group of Chiu Chow followed the two covert field operatives as they left the bar. Each of these Thai number men carried small yet deadly automatic weaponry concealed beneath their jackets.

An airport sanitation employee who was their paid confederate had preplaced the guns in the trash receptacle of the men's room serving the corridor opening on the departure lounge.

Each of the Chiu Chow, in turn, had been paid a large sum of money in exchange for carrying out the mission, with a sizable completion bonus awaiting them at the conclusion of the mission.

That mission was assassination.

Assassination and revenge.

SLATER SENSED that something was wrong when he caught sight of the van accelerating to match speed with the taxi. As it did so, Slater realized that he had seen the van before and understood that its subsequent slowing was no random event.

Moments later he saw the van's side doors trundled quickly open. Even as the ugly black snout of the MAG machine gun jutted through the open hatchway, Slater was yelling at the driver to change lanes.

The taxi driver saw what was happening and reacted quickly. But his actions were those of a panicked man, and he sideswiped a car in the next lane in his wild attempt to evade the black cylinder of death jutting from the open van door.

The result of this hasty action was that the salvo of heavy-caliber rounds that would have struck Deal Slater cut across the driver's side of the taxi instead as the MAG fired a burst a heartbeat later.

The driver's head was stitched open by the jagged line of bullets that crashed through the taxi's windshield.

His body, animated by the impact of the bullets slamming into him, jerked and twitched as though shaken by an invisible fist. The car went out of control and crashed into the embankment at the side of the road.

Bruised but otherwise unhurt, Slater managed to squirm through the door to his right and tumble out onto the dirt. Shock had disoriented him, but the adrenaline was pumping and lifesaving reactions took over.

Slater pulled the Beretta 93-R machine pistol—similar to the M-92 handgun with the addition of a foregrip, muzzle brake and 20-round detachable box magazine—from the pit holster beneath his jacket and threw his outstretched hands across the side of the car in a shooter's grip.

He saw muzzle-flash from the MAG in the van and heard the whining sound of ricocheting heavy-caliber slugs as they bounced off the body of the car and nearby rocks.

Traffic had slowed to a halt, and the van was temporarily trapped. Not for long, though, as Slater saw the driver wrench the wheel and swerve the van across the concrete median divider.

The van was now heading toward his position, but in turning the vehicle, the driver had momentarily placed the gunner's line of sight almost parallel to his position.

Although the machine gunner had swung the barrel full around to the limit of its fire field, the fire would continue to be inaccurate until the van was again flanking its target.

Slater used both the decreasing distance of the van from his position and the wild fire being thrown from the MAG to his advantage.

He could now see the circle of the driver's head behind the windshield.

He sighted along the Beretta at the center of that face, allowing for the deflection of the 9 mm rounds impacting through glass, and squeezed off two bursts in rapid succession, hoping that the windshield was not bulletproof.

It was not.

Split into jagged fracture lines and marked with holes where the bullets had impacted, the windshield was further marred by the sudden blotch of spreading red that had come from the shattered head of the driver.

A moment later the van went racing out of control, careering into the side of a truck that couldn't turn to avoid the collision in time.

Shaky on his feet, Slater watched as gun-toting Chiu Chow spilled from the open doors of the totaled van.

They were carrying Armalites, and although they were as shaken as Slater was, they were recovering their wits quickly. Slater knew that his machine pistol didn't have the range or the firepower to match the 5.56 mm rounds fired by the Armalites.

Snapping off the rest of his clip in a flurry of continuous fire that forced the emerging shooters to tuck their heads down, Slater used the time he had bought to escape from the hit zone.

But even as he reloaded while he ran, he knew that they would follow him relentlessly, for they were Chiu Chow and among the most tenacious killers in the world.

And Deal Slater knew that he might die.

9

The hit crew of Chiu Chow deployed against their targets as Hawke and Bishop were seated in the departure lounge awaiting their flight out of Bangkok.

As soon as the two foreigners were in view, the number men swiftly pulled out their weapons and aimed at their quarry.

With a clear line of fire between his head and the muzzle of the short-bodied autorifle being trained on him, Hawke would have taken lethal hits had not a business traveler suddenly gotten up to stretch his stiffened legs.

At that precise instant the first of the gunmen to raise his weapon triggered a burst of 5.56 mm hollowpoints.

As the rounds impacted and exploded inside him, the businessman flopped backward into the seat he had just vacated. Passengers to either side were covered with blood spewing from the massive wounds in his torso where at least seven slugs had struck in a tightly placed shot pattern.

Seeing the businessman go down and hearing the multiple cracks of automatic gunfire—though knowing little else, including the nature and exact position of the threat in the first instants of engagement—Hawke and Bishop immediately sprang into action.

They knew intuitively that the dead man had caught bullets meant for them. They also knew that the hit coming down at that moment was no random terrorist assault, but a cold-blooded murder attempt. All of this information was apparent on a gut level, instantaneous and galvanizing.

But the shooters had screwed up, and now confusion reigned in the departure lounge with shrieking passengers wildly trying to dodge for any available cover.

As the shooters resighted, Hawke and Bishop pulled out the SIG P-228 semiautomatic pistols they carried and would have taken on the plane, subject to official permits they carried.

Short and light in weight, the SIG packed the stopping power associated with larger-frame handguns.

With the well-honed edge of practiced professionalism, Hawke succeeded in sighting in on one of the shooters who was bringing what looked like a bullpup-configured Valmet M82 into play.

The short-barreled weapon's 5.56 mm rounds and the SIG's parabellum ammo crisscrossed the air, but in the end it was the Valmet-wielding shooter who wound up taking the only hits of the brief but violent exchange.

Dropping his weapon, the gunman went sprawling and tumbling across a row of seats to land face-down in the cushions and one of his legs dangling over the edge.

With one of their number now taken down, a new sense of caution entered the minds of the formerly gung-ho Chiu Chow. The adrenaline edge that had spurred them on was tempered with a newfound constraint in the face of the unanticipated turn the strike had suddenly taken.

Another salvo of combined fire from the two SIG wielded with high accuracy and lightning speed by Hawke and Bishop made the gunmen break for cover. This development gave the SLAM assets a few seconds of safe time in which to move from their crouched position behind the cover of the lounge seats.

Tactical considerations made movement away from ground zero a necessity for survival. To remain where they were would mean giving away the advantage of mobility to the attackers, as well as inviting the possibility of a destabilizing hostage-taking scenario to unfold. Hawke and Bishop needed to move rapidly in order to forestall both potential pitfalls.

The opposition's fire was suppressed temporarily, and Bishop nodded to Hawke while he ejected the spent 15-round magazine from the SIG's handgrip, snapped a fresh magazine into place and cocked the weapon to chamber a fresh parabellum round.

A moment later Hawke was covering Bishop as he went sprinting off toward the departure gate at the opposite end of the lounge, his profile low, his dodging, zigzagging running pattern making him hard to hit.

Keeping low behind the service desk to one side of the gate as his partner moved, Bishop in his turn put out suppressing fire to cover Hawke's escape route.

Bishop emptied his second clip of 9 mm ammo while Hawke, who had reloaded prior to his own move, made a dash across no-man's-land toward the safety of the desk.

Aware of their tactics, the surviving members of the Chiu Chow opposition force reacted by leaning on the triggers of their Valmets.

A hail of 5.56 mm hollowpoints began chewing up the laminated wood surfaces of the desk as Bishop and Hawke threw answering fire at the shooters with the fast-ratcheting autorifles.

Again they used the lull between spasms of automatic fire to break for the departure gate.

Not yet coupled to the accessway hatch of a parked aircraft, the jetway beyond the gate door terminated abruptly about twenty feet above the blacktop of the taxiway located directly below it.

Reaching the end of the short span of truncated jetway, Hawke and Bishop jumped onto the tarmac, rolling after absorbing the impact of the falls with calve and thigh muscles and bringing their weapons up into firing position in practiced, fluid movements.

First on his feet, Bishop tracked the SIG clutched in his fists onto the first of the hitmen who had been brought up short at the end of the jetway and now was pointing the black Valmet bullpup-style auto-weapon down on him.

Two shots in rapid succession tore away most of his lower jaw and sent the shooter and his weapon falling with a dull thud onto the taxiway.

Under a hail of automatic fire, Bishop and Hawke now broke for the nearest source of cover. This happened to be a baggage loader parked on the asphalt nearby.

Reaching the protection of the baggage loader, Hawke covered Bishop while he succeeded in starting the engine of the low-rise vehicle, then climbed aboard to join his partner. By now the three surviving gunmen had also jumped from the gate onto the asphalt and were firing from positions just below the jetway.

Bishop triggered his SIG with one hand as he flattened the accelerator pedal and sent the vehicle hurtling toward the three armed number men at its maximum speed of forty miles per hour.

Two of the Chiu Chow killers were hit by rapidly delivered high-velocity fire from their handguns while the third's bullpup weapon ran dry before he could get out of the way of the onrushing vehicle.

Throwing his arms up over his head in an awkward and futile gesture, the Chiu Chow screamed. But his cry of agony was abruptly cut short as the front end of the baggage loader plowed straight into him at groin level, crushing his body and mangling his limbs beneath its spinning tires.

Hawke and Bishop jumped from the baggage loader just before it crashed into the shooter and struck the terminal wall with a resounding crash. Grasped securely in match grips, their weapons tracked around, seeking target acquisition.

But there were no more shooters in theater.

10

The temple lay just beyond the grove of bamboo that formed a thicket beyond the shoulder of the highway.

Like virtually all other temples in Thailand, the central feature of this one was its ornately carved stupa, the sharply tapering conical structure that ascends symbolically to the realm of the gods and takes with it the spirits of mortal onlookers to their far-flung domain.

But there were also a number of fanciful carvings among the stone edifices that made up the Buddhist temple. These statues of beasts, gods and other deities were often of enormous proportions and were portrayed in the act of dancing, eating, cavorting playfully and even copulating with other gods, avatars and mortal beings.

Slater had no time to play tourist, though. The only thing about the temple that interested him at the present moment was the protection those huge, ancient statues could provide him against the assassination team hot on his heels.

He'd just left the highway a few moments before and needed all the cover he could get. The first of the Chiu Chow shooters was already heading his way, shouting and gesturing as he ran ahead for the other armed number men behind him who had dazedly stumbled from the van to follow his lead.

Reaching the temple after Slater had just gained the cover of a mammoth stone Buddha seated in the traditional lotus position and hunkered behind it, the pursuing mercs ringed the perimeter of the temple.

Fire started blazing from their automatic rifles as they entered the religious sanctuary and spotted their quarry. Slater was outgunned and alone, and each of the pursuers believed that it would only be a matter of persistence and firepower that would decide the ultimate outcome of the engagement.

Slater had other ideas, and he swung up the 93-R machine pistol in answer to the fire pouring down at him from multiple positions on the periphery of the building.

He snapped off three bursts in quick succession as the repeating crack of his bucking gun clashed with the rapid pops of the distant Chiu Chow weapons and the whining of their tumbling 5.56 mm bullets ricocheting off the ancient stone carvings.

Whereas the shooters were going for saturation, Slater's marksmanship proved more effective in retaliating.

He scored himself a hit before the high-capacity magazine in the machine pistol was even half-empty.

The pointman of the four Chiu Chow strikers stumbled as though he had tripped and keeled sideways. The gaping red gash where his left shoulder had been a pulse beat earlier was testament to the fact that he hadn't merely tripped.

Slater snapped off more suppression fire, the 93-R bucking in his hands as he scrambled around the side of the immense Buddha.

The ancient bodhisattva gazed down on the Chiu Chow with the flame-belching weapons at their hips, and his huge carved grey eyes seemed to be brimming with the calm of a soul in nirvanic tranquillity as the number men scrambled forward, hunting their human prey.

Then suddenly a wild card appeared.

From the temple's monk's quarters ran the priest of the temple area. Garbed in the saffron robes of an itinerant monk, the priest waved his arms and shouted for the men to stop their desecration of the holy place by spilling each others' blood.

In answer, the Chiu Chow callously gunned him down. The priest's actions had bought Slater time, though. Scrambling up atop one of the immense statues while their attention was distracted, he sprayed the rest of the strikers with the 93-R studded on full auto before they could get him in their sights.

Struck repeatedly by 3-round pulses of parabellum autofire, the Chiu Chow went down in quick succession. Soon the mortally wounded Chinese number men were lying on the cold ground of the temple.

Slater ran toward the monk whose saffron robes were now crimson with his fast-jetting blood. The old man was still alive, his eyes reflecting a deep inner sorrow at the folly of men who were still fettered by the shackles of earthly ignorance.

Slater heard him utter a phrase in French, the lingua franca of the region, just before he died. He knew enough of that language to understand that the priest was telling him that he was forgiven.

"*Swasdi ka,*" Slater answered as he closed the dead priest's eyes and laid his head gently on the earth. It was Thai for "Peace be with you."

11

Established by the National Security Act of 1947, the National Security Council's mission is defined as follows: it is to assist in crafting national policy by advising the President on issues of national security.

While the key word in the NSC's mandate is *advise,* the council's role has been extended ad hoc in previous administrations to that of something more.

It was from the NSC that special-operations groups were run during the Iran-Contra phase of the Reagan presidency, just as present-day covert paramilitary groups in clandestine support of national policy are run. SLAM was one of these covert paramilitary groups.

On reviewing the decoded satellite telemetry showing the extensive damage caused to the target designated Pivot by the BLU-82 blast, Admiral Harrington, secretary of defense, was ready, willing and able to brief the President on the results of the operation.

One thing that Harrington had learned in his long and distinguished military career was that delivering good news to his superiors made the facts a heck of a lot easier to relate than delivering news not so good.

In this case, the news borne by the admiral was much better than merely good: it was, in fact, almost miraculous.

Having been driven to Andrews Air Force Base by way of the Washington-Baltimore highway loop, Harrington joined the director of central Intelligence and the President's national security adviser and close friend, Yale Enright, for a transcontinental shuttle flight on board *Air Force One*.

It had been noted by the press that the President spent even more time in the air than he did in the Oval Office.

This was more or less true.

The President's hands-on administration policy called upon him to leave Washington far more frequently than had many of his immediate predecessors.

However, he had found that *Air Force One* could be a far more appropriate place for dealing with matters that couldn't be discussed with complete security in the White House, or anywhere else on the ground, for that matter.

Now seated at a table in the electronically sterile conference room of the CinC's executive aircraft, which was at that moment cruising some thirty thousand feet above the midwestern states, the President looked at the three men across the table from him.

Admiral Harrington took the floor as the first speaker to brief the CinC, his visuals and graphics having been digitized and transferred to a videodisc.

This videodisc he placed inside the player in the conference room and directed the attention of the other men to the large-screen television, which sprang to life at a touch of a button on the remote unit held in the admiral's hand.

The President was impressed by the data that his adviser was showing him. The high-visibility strike displayed little in the way of collateral damage. In a word, the bombing results were spectacular.

It was surgical and clean. Better still, its primary purpose, the rescue of a kidnapped Drug Enforcement Administration ground asset, was pristine, one that would play well to the media if and when the need to answer questions ever arose.

Pleased with the results of the covert action, the President wanted more of the same and, furthermore, he wanted it to commence quickly.

The President declared that he would sign an immediate finding forthwith authorizing another covert preemptive strike against the druglords of the Golden Triangle.

It was to commence immediately. And the President was to be informed of the progress of the mission, in terms general enough to provide him with the escape corridor of deniability yet in language that left no doubt as to the depth and scope of the objectives achieved.

12

The U.S. Navy frigate *Fort Worth* rode the vigorous surface chop in a high wind. Lashed to its aft deck, its systems down, was the Pave Low chopper.

With a sudden squall having blown up, the chopper was grounded until such time as weather conditions changed in the Gulf of Thailand, providing more favorable conditions for takeoff.

Slater, Hawke and Bishop didn't like waiting for the operational go-ahead to be given, but they knew how to do it when they had to. Waiting was as much a part of a soldier's lot in life as firing a gun and knowing how to do it was as important a combat skill as any other to develop and master.

While they waited for the weather to clear, they busied themselves checking weapons, commo gear and other specialized equipment.

A breakdown or partial failure of any one of these vital systems in the field could well result in death or capture by the enemy.

Where no declaration of war had been made and no rules of conduct established, being captured could quickly turn out to be far worse an outcome than the relatively quick and clean death by bullet or shrapnel.

The equipment fielded by SLAM was all that stood between the strike team and those it was deployed against, and that equipment had to be better than good, better than excellent.

It had to be *perfect,* or as damned near to it as was humanly possible to achieve.

Slater had disassembled the Spectre SMG that he would be carrying with him on this mission.

As he waited for the go order, he set about recleaning each subassembly of the taken-down weapon and making certain that there was not a speck of dirt or dust present that might clog any of the moveable parts of bolt action, magazine well or receiver.

Hawke checked out the team's PRC-319 HF/VHF burst transmitter unit, as well as other sophisticated portable communications gear on the team's equipment roster, making certain that the hardware and software operated within precisely defined performance parameters and that alkaline batteries, both installed and spares, were all functioning at full power levels.

He also took the opportunity to gain a better familiarity with certain newly established procedures for operating the equipment so that his speed was optimized when he would be called upon to exercise those skills during the course of the operation.

For Eddie Bishop's part, the boredom of waiting had engendered a restlessness that only physical activity could take the edge off.

While his two partners attended to inspecting and maintaining their assorted items of combat matériel, Bishop dropped down to the deck and proceeded to do two hundred push-ups, followed by half that many sit-ups.

At long last the boredom of waiting was finally broken by the announcement over the ship's loudspeaker system that the three covert strikers were to move from below decks to the aft flight deck.

There the military workhorse helicopter known familiarly as the Pave Low was already attached by its shielded power line, which in turn was attached to the dedicated auxiliary power unit, or APU, its powerful engines revving.

Inside the cockpit of the big Pave Low chopper, the pilot and copilot were both going through their predustoff system-check routines. The door gunners were behind their General Electric Miniguns, assuring themselves that these vital weapons and their support systems were in order as the mission manager ran down his own checklist of vital systems.

These tedious ground routines were necessary to establish that all systems were in a condition of peak readiness prior to dustoff. Experience in combat situations had demonstrated time and time again that anything less would not work.

A glitch being discovered would preclude dustoff and ground the chopper for good. The mission would wind up scrubbed.

All systems checked, however, and as the Pave Low's instrument panel chiclets read green all the way, the flight manager hustled the three unconventional-warfare specialists across the flight deck toward the open side hatch of the Pave Low.

Slater, Hawke and Bishop jumped inside the big Pave Low chopper and took their places along the bulkheads, each snapping on the safety tether that crew members wore when in flight.

Along with them were the two gunners who manned the two GE Miniguns with which the big, but maneuverable helicopter was equipped. The Miniguns were advanced, electrically actuated Gatling machine guns that fired thousands of rounds of 7.62 mm NATO standard ammunition.

Soon the chopper had crossed the sea and was hovering above the tree line of the southern portion of Thailand a few kilometers inland from the beach.

Invisible to radar by maneuvering at treetop level in a nap-of-the-earth navigational pattern, the Pave Low was nevertheless as slow as it was big compared to conventional fixed-wing aircraft.

Concealment and stealth instead of firepower was what the crew of the Pave Low counted on to get the chopper to its target zone and back to base again.

Under cover of night, the pilot navigated the big bird by means of the AN/PVS-8 forward-looking infrared display.

The color graphics display on the console FLIR view screen allowed him a high-definition view of the terrain the Pave Low overflew on its course toward its destination, which was several hundred kilometers inland.

The flight took over an hour to complete. At the end of the run the pilot's voice came crisply over the rotorcraft's intercom. He announced that the gunners should man their weapons stations.

The GE Miniguns unsafed, the door gunners in their bullet-resistant flak vests and Kevlar helmets looked down across the jungle tree line, alert for signs of human activity that didn't belong there.

The clearing where SLAM was to be inserted into the operations zone was visible now as the Pave Low descended, its rotor dishing.

There was still no overt sign of hostiles in the LZ, but appearances could be deceiving and the crew continued to remain in a high state of readiness.

Attackers could be concealed in the bushes, waiting for helicraft to touch down before opening up. Or the land surface could be laced with mines that could be set off by the touch of a chopper's skids or the pressure of a combat soldier's boot.

In any event the pilot of the big chopper had no intention of touching the chopper down.

As soon as he considered the clearing secure, he brought the mammoth whirlybird to within a few feet of the ground and issued the command for the three covert warriors to jump out of the helicraft's yawning rear hatch. Slater took the lead, then covered Hawke and Bishop as they descended from the helicraft.

Turning their backs to the gunship, the three strikers vanished into the jungle as the Pave Low immediately lifted off from the LZ, its Minigun barrels continuing to track the clearing even as it ascended into the blackness of a moonless night.

The pilot and copilot exchanged glances when the Pave Low had cleared the tree line and was in position to fly away from the drop zone.

They were glad to be airborne again and on their way back across the jungle to the safety of the frigate, although in a part of their minds they envied the men they had just placed on the ground.

13

The covert strike team moved slowly and silently through the dense jungle. The trail they followed meandered through stands of bamboo, and thick underbrush crowded in from either side. The jungle terrain was typical of Southeast Asia—lush and green and moist with the triple-tiered canopy overhead.

The strike team's land navigation function was conducted principally by means of a compact Magellan GPS unit.

A unique piece of field equipment, the hand-held device, equipped with its pop-up antenna, had rendered the compass as obsolete as the calculator had rendered the slide rule.

Electronically uplinked to a phased array of Navstar satellites sweeping around the earth in a geosynchronous orbit, the GPS units were capable of pinpointing anywhere on the globe to within a few feet of its actual location.

Their twenty-column, ten-line backlit liquid-crystal digital display panel displayed waypoints to the chosen objective, as well as position data calibrated in latitude and longitude.

Taking the Magellan from one of the pouches riding his load-bearing suspenders, Mason Hawke at once proceeded to verify the team's progress toward its mission objective.

The global positioner unit indicated that the target zone was no more than two kilometers from their present position. Additionally Hawke confirmed that the strike team was moving toward its destination and was not deviating from its intended line of march by any strategically significant margin.

What the GPS unit did not say was the exact nature of the destination itself. This data resided inside the brains of the individuals who comprised the SLAM unit, as did the knowledge of the parts that each member of the team would play during the course of the action to come.

The mission objective was a ruined Buddhist temple complex—code-named Back Door—that was nestled in the heart of the jungle. As its designation implied, taking out the target would almost be like closing down a thief's entrance to Kuhn Sa's heroin empire.

Wat Lamphun was not a contemporary structure. The inhabitants of the area have been putting up temples for centuries, and many lie in ruins to the present day. These ancient holy sites are quickly covered by fast-growing jungle until they disappear completely from view.

Back Door was such a place.

The temple had been constructed in the fifth century A.D. by monks who had trekked down from India and had fallen into disuse hundreds of years later. The ruins, cut off by dense jungle from the nearest village in the rugged mountain terrain, were not in any way used for the purpose for which they had originally been intended.

No supplicants worshiped at the weathered stone shrines, and no offerings of incense, flowers or coins were laid at the crossed legs of the bodhisattva figure that had been carved long ago by unnamed monk-artisans as a celebration of religious transcendence and the freedom from earthly ignorance.

Instead, Wat Lamphun sheltered activities that were a direct antithesis of those worshiping the peaceful gods of the Buddhist religious pantheon. In recent months Intelligence analysis had made it plain that Wat Lamphun was the center of a massive opium transshipment and processing operation.

The temple was a very important part of Kuhn Sa's heroin empire and a source of millions of dollars of illicit narcodollars that enriched the coffers of the druglord. The heroin processed at the temple's laboratories found its way onto the streets of U.S. cities, making the processing cite a prime target for destruction.

After they had marched for several hours through the dark jungle, Hawke, who was on point, held up his hand, indicating that the Magellan unit had pinpointed their location as right on the site. The NVGs worn by the team illuminated the jungle surroundings as they stopped and prepared to conduct their initial reconnaissance.

Slater and Hawke stood guard while Bishop went ahead to recon the strike perimeter. In front of him he could now see the temple framed in the bright green view field of his goggles.

There was activity in the ruined Buddhist shrine as flickering fires from smudge pots burned to provide heat and light for those within its confines. An assortment of vehicles were parked in the compound, and lights shone down into the interior of the place from high stanchions.

After scanning the terrain to left and right and establishing that no hostile forces were present in the vicinity, Bishop went back to his two teammates and reported on the situation to them.

Once they had received Bishop's all clear, Slater and Hawke proceeded to the forward observation area from which they, too, could have the opportunity to conduct a probe of the temple.

BEFORE ANY ACTION was taken, a phase of waiting and watching the strike area was adopted.

First the SLAM detail dug spider holes into which they could drop down and shelter throughout their vigil. These holes were camouflaged with jungle vegetation against detection by unfriendlies and they also afforded defensible positions in the event of a firefight.

Throughout the rest of the night, they viewed the strike zone from their concealed location within the spider holes.

What they were after was an assessment of activity patterns in addition to information about strong points and weak points of the area. This data would permit Slater to craft a strike plan that would potentially inflict maximum damage on the target site.

Their night-vision goggles provided the SLAM strike team with excellent viewing conditions even in the complete darkness of a moonless jungle night.

Reconnoitering the target from the stationary positions of their spider holes was supplemented by timed mobile recons, as well. Each of the three strikers was scheduled to go out on one of these missions every few hours.

By these operational methods, the strike team was able to map into memory a three-dimensional picture of the base and its patterns of activity. This would be necessary for a subwarfare unit that fought in three dimensions, employing stealth, speed and firepower to confuse and confound the enemy while dealing it a series of deadly punches.

Soon the darkness had started to give way to a hazy gray dawn, and each of the team members knew that before their recon phase was over, they would develop a strong sense of how best to take the base and inflict the maximum possible level of violence on it and its occupants.

An extra edge for their small but deadly operation was the fact that nobody inside the base had any inkling that crouching in the dark jungle outside the heroin-processing station were the agents of swift, sure termination brought silently their way from a distant land.

14

It was 0450 hours, and the SLAM team moved in on the target stealthily, speedily and deliberately.

Slater took the point.

In his hands he held the SITES Spectre SMG, its fire-selection lever studded on full auto, a 9 mm round in its firing chamber and forty-nine more waiting to be called upon for action in its high-capacity clip.

Slater checked his wrist chronometer with a quick glance at the dial. In twenty seconds he would receive the signal to move on his objective.

Across the compound the charges they had planted during the course of the night were all set to detonate in rapid, phased pulses primed to deliver a punishing flurry of blows to the encampment.

But as devastating as their effects would be, the C-4 charges were mostly diversionary in nature. Delivering the real damage was the responsibility of the strike team.

When the zeros on the digital display of Slater's chronometer lined up, the charges blew. Blinding white detonation flashes strobed through the canopy of dense jungle palm trees. The flash was accompanied by the thunder of high-explosive munitions going off, seemingly everywhere at once.

The explosions produced the desired effect, Slater could see at a glance.

The sentries walking their perimeters along the wire were the first to be drawn toward the scene of the sudden, convulsing blasts. Although they wore jungle O.D.s and carried the AK-series autorifles, which had become a familiar sight in the operations zone, they could hardly be termed professional soldiers.

Their reactions were those of amateurs who allowed themselves to be drawn toward the diversion, sucked in by the enemy's well-crafted offensive strategy.

Slater held up his hand as he watched these destabilized forces shout and mill about, thrown completely off balance, as the flames licked high into the sky. He was waiting for more troops to join the tin soldiers already exposed in the open.

This happened in moments as more troops spilled out of the barracks building inside Back Door's perimeter. Slater now issued rapid instructions to his men, calling for the kill trap to be sprung on the enemy soldiers.

The .50-caliber Barret machine guns set up on bipod legs had been sited in order to produce a crisscross effect. The advanced-design Barrets were lightweight and specially modified to accept a 100-round box magazine.

Once the unfriendlies were massed at the end of the temple compound nearest to the munitions diversion, Slater judged that conditions were optimum to produce a maximum kill ratio.

At Slater's signal, Hawke and Bishop opened up with the .50-caliber Barrets, the deep, rhythmic thudding of the heavy-caliber ammunition echoing through the night as glowing green tracers crisscrossed through the darkness.

Caught by surprise, the troops sustained heavy casualties as the .50-caliber rounds struck their targets in a concentrated wall of whirlwinding automatic fire.

Slater saw the first of the victims of the withering fire drop and stay put where he fell. More of the temple's armed defenders went down in the first few seconds of the surprise burst, which had found them completely unprepared.

The remainder of the base personnel recovered in the initial seconds of the skilfully and speedily executed surprise attack.

Although shocked and disoriented, their reflexes took over and the paramilitary troops sighted on the muzzle-flashes of the flame-bratting Barret machine guns.

But the response of these scattered forces was mechanical and spiritless, motivated more from fear than from sound tactical considerations.

The result of this debacle was a display of answering fire whose wild and undisciplined character showed that the troops were already beaten men whether they realized it yet or not.

Slater wasn't about to give the men the chance to regroup or gain an iota of initiative.

After the first pulse of automatic heavy-caliber fire, he raised to his shoulder the multiple LAW rocket launcher that he had unshipped from his gear pack. Sighting in on the center of the mass of survivors, he triggered the first of the four rounds contained in the multiple launcher.

The high-explosive antitank warhead impacted seconds later, its charge and prefragmented shrapnel exploding and taking a deadly toll. The second, third and fourth warheads followed suit, exacting even more carnage as they struck and detonated.

With the defenders now reduced in numbers, Slater set down the spent LAW tube and took up the Spectre SMG that hung on its elasticized TEAM combat sling from his shoulders. Hawke and Bishop followed suit, hefting their lightweight Barret advanced-design machine guns.

Together they stormed the base.

The carnage that the SLAM crew's surprise attack had left in its bloody wake was nearly total, but nevertheless there were stragglers who had survived the onslaught.

These came running from the various stone structures that comprised the architecture of the temple, but most of them were bent on escape rather than confrontation.

Slater sighted the Spectre on two paramilitary troopers who were struggling to start up a Nissan truck and hustle from the firezone. Two long bursts of parabellums from hip-fire position took down the one on the passenger side of the vehicle before he could bring his autoweapon into firing position.

Seeing his partner topple from the now-moving truck, the driver pulled a pistol from a chest rig and pointed it at Slater. But Slater had already dodged to one side and now raked the truck with sustained automatic fire from the Spectre SMG, whose high-capacity 50-round magazine contained plenty of ammunition for the task at hand.

Reloading a fresh magazine into the Spectre as the driver went sprawling from the open-topped vehicle, Slater raced toward the first objective, the heroin-processing laboratory of the temple, leaving Hawke and Bishop to carry out the final mopping-up phase of the hard penetration of the clandestine jungle drug base.

Slater heard the thudding of SLAM's big guns as he hurried inside and assessed the tactical situation confronting him. He could tell at a glance that the heroin-processing lab was sophisticated in its setup.

Slater slotted plastic explosive charges throughout the drug lab, determined to ensure that the destruction would be comprehensive. Inserting detonator caps into the puttylike blasting material, he linked these to their timers and set each timer's digital readout for five minutes.

In minutes he was joined by Bishop and Hawke.

"The opposition is all put away," Hawke reported to Slater. "The base is secure."

But Hawke had apparently spoken too soon. Hardly had the words come out of his mouth than a paramilitary popped out from behind a weathered and time-stained stone carving of Manjusri, a divine personage wielding a sword astride a lion, and whipped out a small but mean-looking SMG.

The shooter was fast but not nearly fast enough to put his quarry away. The silenced Spectre in Slater's fist spoke with wheezing cough, delivering its death sentence with a fiery whisper, and the attacker dropped to the ground to crimson it with his blood.

"What was that you said about secure?" Slater asked Hawke, whose only response was to shake his head in chagrin.

With the last of the opposition's number down, Slater and his crew rushed out of the compound of the jungle drug lab. Before they left the temple behind, Bishop booby-trapped the bodies of the downed troops with trembler bombs.

The mercury switches linked to the explosive charges placed beneath the bodies were sensitive to the slightest motion. The circuit would close as soon as anyone disturbed the bodies, adding more kills to the rising body count and ensuring that the enemy got the message that SLAM brought loud and clear: mess with the best, die like the rest.

Its work completed, SLAM proceeded stealthily from the strike zone. The team hustled quickly into the surrounding jungle and were well within the protection of the tree line as the charges in the drug lab blew with a tremendous report behind them.

The night turned into day for a moment as the detonation flash lit up the surroundings.

But SLAM wasn't just hustling to distance themselves from ground zero. They also wanted to make sure they were out of the area before any hostiles surrounded them—hostiles put on alert by the thunder and lightning of explosions that had swept like a storm of vengeance through the jungle night.

PART TWO:

Under Fire

15

Before any observers could arrive at the site of the explosion, SLAM was already many klicks away from the scene of the clandestine strike. Their jungle craft was up to the task of land navigation under combat conditions, aided considerably by the Magellan units that the strike team fielded on its recon by fire.

Because of the success of the first strike, which had come off both flawlessly and quickly, Deal Slater had decided that SLAM would opt to carry out a strike on their secondary target, code-named Coffee House, in addition to the strike on the ruined temple.

Coffee House was another important juncture of Kuhn Sa's sprawling heroin empire lying to the north of their first strike, code-named Back Door. Unlike Wat Lamphun, however, Coffee House was a drug transshipment point rather than a lab and processing center per se.

Across its crude airstrip, drug-laden planes made regular landings and takeoffs, flying hundreds of tons of opium base and processed heroin out of the jungle annually to destinations all over Southeast Asia.

Having reached a suitable stopping point some ten klicks from the temple, Slater ordered a rest break during which he would make contact with Convention and inform the mission support facility on board the Navy frigate *Forth Worth* that the strike team was proceeding to their secondary target.

This communication would be established by burst transmitter. The unit available to SLAM in the field was a Philips PRC-319 HF/VHF, similar in size and shape to a notebook computer although in a milspec hardened shell and with a capacity to compress a typed message sixty-four kilobytes in length into a pulsed, encrypted signal barely a second in duration.

Because the unit was programmed to transmit its signal to a Vortex-class Intelligence satellite launched by the National Security Agency and currently orbiting the earth in a wide-apogee circumpolar orbit, Slater had timed the rest break to coincide with the window of opportunity for transmission that now prevailed.

Unshipping the PRC-319 from its shockproof pouch stowed in his rucksack, Slater sat on a rock, placed the covert transmission unit atop his lap and pulled back its lid to position its liquid-crystal digital-display panel.

He initialized the unit and began to input data at the keyboard when prompted by the screen.

The message he typed concisely at the keyboard stated that the search-locate-annihilate team had successfully taken down the heroin-processing center at the target designated Back Door.

It stated, as well, that SLAM would now proceed to redeploy and carry out an interdictive strike at the drug-transshipment site bearing the secret code descriptor Coffee House.

Having completed entering his situation report and battle-damage assessment at the burst transmitter's console, Slater proofread the text and saved the data to CMOS memory.

The sophisticated unit performed an encryption subroutine as its automatic save operation ran. With this procedure having been duly completed, Slater then exited the text-editor mode and chained to the unit's send menu.

Among the menu's options were the time-delay factor before the burst message was transmitted. Consulting his digital wrist chronometer, Slater selected a fifteen-second delay and set the unit to erase the message upon transmission.

Fifteen seconds later, as the unit's supertwist LCD screen informed him that it was transmitting the encrypted message, a Vortex Intelligence platform at orbital perigee received the burst and stored it in its own microprocessor memory.

Using appropriate handshaking protocols, the ground- and space-based devices confirmed that the transmission had been carried out successfully.

As Slater's compact unit issued him the confirm message, the multiton Vortex Intelsat was already in the process of beaming the message stored in its silicon memory down to the Navy frigate *Fort Worth* standing by in the Gulf of Thailand.

This telemetry would also be encrypted in a manner virtually impossible to decipher by even the most powerful computer in the world without the appropriate software key in the possession of the personnel at the receiving station on the ground.

Having transmitted the message, Slater stowed the unit away in his rucksack and instructed Hawke and Bishop to get ready to move out again.

Both members of the elite strike team ported their .50-caliber machine guns as they moved stealthily through the jungle via the narrow trail, their NVGs showing them a brightly illuminated field of view despite the utter blackness of the jungle night.

HAD DEAL SLATER or his men been aware of the events taking place several klicks beyond their area of operations in a fertile valley in the Shan Mountains, they might not have chosen to go after their secondary target and opted for a helicopter extraction instead.

But they could have not possessed any knowledge of the fact that a response to the armed strike team operating in the jungle had already been crafted and set into motion.

In a bamboo hut that served as Kuhn Sa's command headquarters, the commander of the Shan United Army was slamming his balled fist down on the table as he faced his lieutenants.

"These men are American commandos, maybe Green Berets," Kuhn Sa shouted, the muscles on his lean face flexing in a way that his lieutenants knew might prove highly dangerous if they did not handle the situation correctly. "I have asked you to deal with them. How have you?"

"General," the first of Kuhn Sa's lieutenants, a man named Dao Lin, said as he rose from the table. "We have already set events into motion. Two companies of our troops have been assembled. They are scheduled to deploy into the jungle within a matter of hours. They are making final checks on their weapons at this moment."

Dao was pleased to note that his remarks had something of a mollifying effect on Kuhn Sa, apparent by the relaxing of his facial muscles and the fading of the dangerous gleam from his hooded eyes.

"Who will lead the men?"

"I will personally lead one of the companies," Dao replied. "My esteemed peer, Colonel Sung, will lead the other company. You may rest assured that the Americans—as you are almost certainly correct in assuming that the interlopers are—will be dealt with."

Kuhn Sa regarded the speaker for a long moment, his eyes darting to the man seated beside the standing Dao, whose face was set resolutely.

Yes, Kuhn Sa thought, Sung was truly a gifted field commander, a soldier whom he had schooled himself in the arts of guerrilla warfare and jungle craft. And Dao had spoken confidently and well.

"I know that you and Sung will not let me down," Kuhn Sa said to his lieutenants. "But I want my revenge total!" he continued, hammering his bunched fist onto the tabletop, his voice suddenly raised to a deafening level.

"Bring me their heads!" he shouted. "Or do not bother to return at all!"

16

Coffee House appeared to be a soft target, highly vulnerable to an interdiction strike.

As SLAM scoped out the mission zone from the cover of the jungle tree line through GEN III NVGs, they saw that the covert jungle landing strip was manned by a force of no greater strength than a skeleton crew of Chiu Chow.

As Slater, Hawke and Bishop reconnoitered the area, though, they realized that they had been handed an unexpected bonus. This might wind up being a surprise gift that might make their task of smashing the base a whole lot easier to accomplish.

On the landing field was a DC-6 four-engine cargo aircraft capable of flying a twelve-ton payload over twenty-one hundred miles. The plane, a veteran of a substantial number of drug runs from the looks of its dented and weatherbeaten hull, was at that moment in the process of being loaded up with a cargo of raw opium base.

Chiu Chow guards armed with AK and the shorter-barreled AKRs stood watching the work-men—distinguishable from their overseers by the absence of Rolex watches and ostentatious gold jewelry, which was a hallmark of the number-men dress code—load the pallets of semirefined drug product into the hold of the plane.

A shack made of slatted hardwood with a variety of antennae bristling from its irregular, sloping tin roof stood at the perimeter of the landing strip.

Leaning against the side of the shack was a male Westerner well dressed in a khaki bush jacket ensemble. He was probably the pilot of the aircraft.

He was speaking with another man, dressed in the manner of the Chiu Chow, who was probably the equivalent of the station manager, since he was armed only with a pistol worn at his belt in a black leather holster and kept a close eye on the loading operation.

Again the stopping power of the .50-caliber Barret machine guns ported by Hawke and Bishop would cover Slater on point, bringing down the base support personnel as SLAM split their defenses like an iron wedge driven into a block of wood.

The Barrets were loaded with tracers every fourth bullet on the feed belt. This arrangement not only gave the two squad gunners the availability of accurately taping their quarry, but also created an effect resembling a luminous stream of deadly green fire, lancing down like a lethal bolt cast by angry gods.

On Slater's orders, the fire team unsafed their weapons and opened up on the airstrip's sentries.

Struck by heavy-caliber autofire, two went down almost immediately.

The psychological effect of the tracer loads enhanced the terror that the sudden appearance of three armed commandos from out of the dark jungle had on the men at Coffee House.

While some of the Chiu Chow guards summoned up enough courage to put up a halfhearted resistance, others broke and ran at the sight of the terrifying apparitions that had fallen on them like the legendary *phi bop* from the jungle.

But in the end it didn't matter very much which option—cowardice or belligerence—the targeted drug runners chose in the face of the commando strike detail's hammering onslaught.

SLAM's withering firepower sought them all out and mowed them down as though the opposition were stalks of wheat falling beneath the flailing scythe of the grim reaper.

Those who ran away instead of holding their ground succeeded only in living a few seconds longer than they might have otherwise. But these were seconds of terror as deadly specters sought them in the vortexing maw of the ruptured night.

At the narrow apex of the assault wedge, Slater raced toward the communications center of the jungle aircraft landing strip.

He had seen the two men speaking there dive for cover and go off in opposite directions as soon as the first salvo of autofire was heard and the first flame-belching muzzle-flash from the big guns seen, indicating a full-out assault.

The Chinese had ducked into the doorway while the man whom Slater suspected of being the pilot of the DC-6 had made a desperate dash for the cockpit of the plane that was being prepared for takeoff.

"Take the plane," Slater spoke into the rice-grain microphone of the AN/PRC comsets. "I'll hit the radio shack."

"That's affirm," Slater heard both Hawke and Bishop respond to his transmission as he braced himself along the side of the doorway to the radio shack.

For the moment letting the Spectre SMG fall to his side on the elasticized combat sling, Slater pulled two miniflashbangs from the fastenings on which they hung from his combat suspender.

Holding the two grenades in his tactical-gloved fists, Slater drove the sole of his jump boot solidly into the middle of the makeshift structure's flimsy wooden door.

It flew open, and Slater tossed in the two stun grenades, which immediately detonated, producing blinding magnesium flashes and a series of deafening explosions.

Just behind the flashbangs, Slater swept into the room beyond the door on a half roll, coming up with the Spectre in his fists in the center of the plank floor.

Although his quarry was disoriented by the flashbangs, he still held on to his small black automatic pistol and tried to aim at the fast-moving, side-breaking target that had stormed through the door.

While holding the microphone of a transmitter unit to his mouth and shouting rapidly into it, he squeezed off several shots in quick succession at the baleful apparition stalking through smoke, noise and flash.

But the radioman was trying to transmit his desperate message, and spots swam before his eyes and alarms rang in his ears from the detonations, and his aim was off.

Slater had no intention to give the radioman the opportunity to improve his aim.

From a half crouch, he targeted the Spectre and squeezed off a long burst of fast-rotoring parabellums. The 9 mm slugs spewed from the flame-belching muzzle of the SMG and stitched the radioman high across the chest in a butterfly of scything steel.

The effect of the simultaneous multiple bullet impacts in close-in, "room-cleaning" style adapted by Slater was dramatic.

The man suddenly began trembling all over with the fidgety animation of a puppet jerked by unseen strings as blood sprayed from his body under the wallop of the high-velocity slugs.

As the takedown went sprawling from his seat, Slater wasted no more of his ammo on the radio equipment.

Pulling two frag submunitions from his suspenders, he tossed them under the table supporting the blood-spattered radio equipment as he ducked back out through the door of the radio shack.

It blew behind him moments later with a thunderous report, sending scorching tongues of flame off into the night behind the fast-sprinting shadow warrior.

Emerging from the radio shack, Slater could see that Bishop and Hawke were going after the DC-6, which was in the process of taxiing for a short-runway takeoff.

The pilot's chances of getting the DC-6 into the air in time to escape the killing were not very good, but awareness of the grave consequences of being caught on the ground had made him more than willing to give it a try.

The commandos were taking no prisoners, the pilot had seen. They were only beefing up the body count as much as possible.

Jutting the snout of a MAC-11 SMG through the cockpit window, the pilot got off most of the rounds in the compact autoweapon's 32-round clip while he gave the crate everything it had.

But neither skill nor luck could combine to save the pilot's neck. Hawke and Bishop had the range and firepower, thanks to their .50-caliber Barret squad weapons, to blow him to hell and gone and back again if necessary.

PLAY "LUCKY HEARTS" AND GET...

★ **4 Hard-hitting, action-packed Gold Eagle novels — FREE**
★ **PLUS a surprise mystery gift — FREE**

THEN CONTINUE YOUR LUCKY STREAK WITH A SWEETHEART OF A DEAL

1. Play Lucky Hearts as instructed on the opposite page.

2. Send back the card and you'll get hot-off-the-press Gold Eagle books, never before published. These books have a total cover price of $15.49, but they are yours to keep absolutely free.

3. There's no catch. You're under no obligation to buy anything. We charge nothing – ZERO – for your first shipment. And you don't have to make any minimum number of purchases – not even one!

4. The fact is thousands of readers enjoy receiving books by mail from the Gold Eagle Reader Service. They like the convenience of home delivery. . . they like getting the best new novels before they're available in stores. . . and they love our discount prices!

5. We hope that after receiving your free books you'll want to remain a subscriber. But the choice is yours – to continue or cancel, anytime at all! So why not take us up on our invitation, with no risk of any kind. You'll be glad you did!

SURPRISE MYSTERY GIFT COULD BE YOURS **FREE** WHEN YOU PLAY LUCKY HEARTS

GOLD EAGLE'S
LUCKY HEARTS

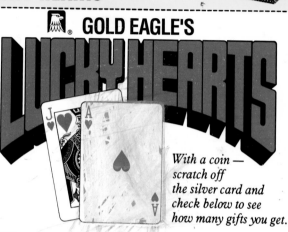

With a coin — scratch off the silver card and check below to see how many gifts you get.

YES! I have scratched off the silver card. Please send me the books and gift for which I qualify. I understand that I am under no obligation to purchase any books, as explained on the back and on the opposite page.

164 CIM AKY5
(U-SLM-08/93)

NAME

ADDRESS   APT.

CITY   STATE   ZIP

Twenty-one gets you 4 free books, and a free mystery gift

Twenty gets you 4 free books

Nineteen gets you 3 free books

Eighteen gets you 2 free books

Offer limited to one per household and not valid to present subscribers. All orders subject to approval.

PRINTED IN U.S.A.

©1993 Gold Eagle

THE GOLD EAGLE READER SERVICE : HERE'S HOW IT WORKS

Accepting free books puts you under no obligation to buy anything. You may keep the books and gift and return the shipping statement marked "cancel." If you do not cancel, about a month later we will send you four additional novels and bill you just $13.80* – that's a saving of over 10% off the cover price of all four books! And there's no extra charge for shipping! You may cancel at any time, but if you choose to continue, then every other month we'll send you four more books, which you may either purchase at the discount price... or return at our expense and cancel your subscription.

*Terms and prices subject to change without notice. Sales tax applicable in N.Y.

Pouring fire at the fast-moving plane, Hawke and Bishop's twin lines of green tracers converged on the DC-6's tail assembly. Puncturing the riveted hull and penetrating the four-engine plane's fuel tanks, the glowing tracers set off the high-octane aviation gasoline that the tanks had been filled to capacity with prior to takeoff.

A roaring explosion engulfed the stricken aircraft almost instantly as the rounds ignited the fuel. The DC-6 broke in two as a result, and the ball of fire that rose from the plane widened in an eye blink, throwing the pilot clear of the cockpit.

Although he'd been thrown clear, the pilot was doused with aviation fuel, and the thrashing, flame-wreathed form that flailed through the air and lay convulsed on the ground, screaming and howling, had no chance of survival.

A burst from Hawke's .50-caliber squad weapon silenced the pilot's final agonies before the flames in which he was cocooned could consume his life.

In the eerie stillness that slowly settled on the burning strike target in the aftermath of the spasm of destruction visited on it by its night-masked attackers, Deal Slater stood and assessed the damage to the target code-named Coffee House.

Damage was total.

17

"Wait one. I see movement on the Sector Bravo," Slater heard Hawke say in his earpiece. "I say again, I see movement on the Sector Bravo."

Having moved quickly on extraction from Coffee House, the SLAM commando team was now mobilized several kilometers from the fire-ravaged target in the final hour before twilight.

The team still wore its NVGs, due to the darkness that prevailed beneath the shroud of the forest canopy.

Navigating the land in a triangle formation, each member of the unconventional-warfare strike unit was orbiting some thirty meters equilaterally from one another. Hawke was taking the point this time, with Slater and Bishop forming the end points of the base of the triangle to Hawke's rear flanks.

After having taken out Coffee House, the strike team had fulfilled all parameters of its interdiction strike mission.

The team had successfully destroyed a drug-trafficking infrastructure that would require many months or even years to build back up to the level that it had been at when hit.

The lightning assault had also resulted in the deaths of a large number of trained, veteran personnel. These losses, too, would be difficult to replace and restructure. And in a business where time was on the side of established power bases, the blow would be significant to Kuhn Sa.

Finally the strike had also destroyed millions of dollars' worth of raw and semirefined narcotics product, resulting both in a net financial loss to the drug cartels, which profited from refinement and distribution of the contraband in the high six figures.

Most importantly the success of the strikes ensured that significantly smaller quantities of the poison, which men like Kuhn Sa referred to by the deceptively innocent-sounding title of "the white powder," would not reach the veins of drug users and would-be drug users in America, Europe and elsewhere.

The destination of the strike team, as it deployed through the jungle in the aftermath of the hit on Coffee House, was its rally point for linkup and extraction via the heavy hauling Pave Low helicopter that had ferried SLAM into the operations zone some forty-eight hours before.

From the rally point the heavily armored military gunship would fly them via an overland route across the mountainous spine of Thailand to the coast and across the Gulf of Thailand for an RV with the waiting frigate.

At the moment that Slater and Bishop received Hawke's sudden warning betokening unfriendlies in the area, the covert-mission detail had progressed roughly midway toward the designated rally point.

Slater immediately issued orders for the team to establish the nature of the force on their flank, whether it was following the commando team and what its numbers were before taking any action.

In the main this duty fell to Bishop who dropped back to gather Intelligence on the sighting while Slater and Hawke, changing their line of march, proceeded at a brisk pace toward high ground from which they might stage an ambush if it was deemed necessary to do so.

From a position of concealment amid a pile of lichen-encrusted granite boulders overlooking the line of the unknown force's march, Bishop saw that the force was made up of about thirty men. This would make it at roughly company level in strength from all appearances, although there was the possibility that more personnel were in the area beyond his field of view.

As Bishop continued to surveil the force from his covert vantage point, the uniformed soldier acting as scout stopped and inspected the ground at his feet. The rest of the column behind him also halted at a signal from the group's leader, allowing the scout to perform his duties.

Carefully running his eye along the forest floor, the scout nodded to himself as a man might when confirming an inwardly held supposition. When he straightened again he spoke rapidly to the older man who was undoubtedly the commander of the force, emphatically gesturing and pointing ahead of him.

To Bishop these activities confirmed that the force was indeed tracking the American commando raiders in a deliberate effort to hunt them down before they reached their rally point. There was no question in his mind that the paramilitaries were out to kill rather than capture.

Bishop, familiar with land navigation methods used in the jungle tactical environment, was also familiar with the techniques that the scout at the head of the column was employing.

He had no doubt that the man was good at what he did. The locals in any given vicinity usually were. Rarely did they not make formidable trackers when they could be trusted to serve the interests of the mission.

"Listen up," Bishop said into the rice-grain mike of his comset. "Hostile force of double-company strength. Are tracking our progress."

"That's affirm," Slater said back. "Proceed to map coordinates Baker-Talon-Echo-Four."

"I copy you," Bishop replied as he punched up the coordinates on his hand-held Magellan global positioning unit, its LCD readout immediately translating the position sited into precise distance and compass-point readings.

SLAM WAS NOW TAKING evasive action in an attempt to determine if they could shake off pursuit.

But although they were using false breaks to the side, creating trail diversions by covering their tracks and utilizing the entire bag of tricks of the jungle fighter's field craft, the pursuing force was still closing in.

With time a critical factor, Slater decided that the team's only option at that point lay in setting up a kill trap.

He selected high ground overlooking the bed of a dry stream. It paralleled the natural course that the pursuing force would take in its hunt for the commando raiders in the area, and Slater further enhanced the bait by deliberately leaving spoor behind.

This was in the form of a shred from a field ration wrapper and a bit of torn fabric caught on projecting branches—branches that had been snapped now and again to signal undisciplined troops moving quickly through the brush out of haste or fear of pursuit.

As the team set up its heavy-caliber squad guns in preparation for the kill trap, the lure placed in the opposition's path began to draw them in.

With General Dao in the lead of his company of troops, the body of men threaded its way down, not suspecting that they were being led to their deaths.

Slater waited until they were all inside the kill trap, then he triggered the first of the claymores he had placed at the front of the gully.

The claymore detonated, blowing hundreds of steel balls at the first of the men to enter the trap. As expected, those at the center and rear ran backward, only to be forced back in the direction they had come by the detonation of the second phased claymore from the rear.

But there was no place to run to except into the flesh-rending cross fire of steel balls set up by the two last claymores positioned across from each other on either bank of the gully.

These final bursts razored through the force and killed the stragglers. In the brief space of a few minutes, all members of the pursuing company were dead.

Bishop covered Slater and Hawke, while they scrambled down the bank to inspect the kills. A quick search of the bodies revealed that apart from personal effects they carried no papers of extraordinary value.

Slater motioned for Bishop to come down from the high ground, and the three commandos set off again toward their rally point with the Pave Low, all members of the strike team now cognizant of the fact that they were running behind schedule.

They didn't know that a few dozen klicks between themselves and the rally point a second company dispatched by Kuhn Sa, under the command of Colonel Sung, was moving toward their position, having heard the explosions of the claymores that had destroyed the other force.

18

The first inkling SLAM had that they were cut off from reaching the team's helicopter RV was at the point where they made visual contact with the second company of pursuing Shan United Army troops moving toward them across a jungle-canopied ridge.

The firefight broke out as the opposition forces made contact with their quarry, tearing the twilight asunder.

Suddenly finding themselves under heavy automatic fire, the commandos split up and took evasive action. Each of the team's three members now fought for his life against heavy odds.

Splitting up not only had the tactical effect of disorienting the pursuing body of men and forcing them to divide their own numbers three ways, but also increased the odds of at least one of the SLAM team members surviving to make it out of the firezone.

By this point it was already too late for them to reach the assigned rally point in time to meet the aircraft.

Furthermore, the crew of the Pave Low chopper had direct and uncontravenable orders to withdraw from the area immediately if they did not see the infrared strobes that SLAM were to activate as landing beacons prior to extraction.

Slater had scouted out two fallback positions for the team as required by field craft, and it was to one of these positions, assigned the code name Razor, that the team members were to head for if they succeeded in evading the pursuing force hot on their trail.

WHILE SLAM WAS TAKING fire in the game of deadly hide-and-seek they were playing with their determined pursuers, the Pave Low chopper was undertaking the final leg of its NOE flight vector toward its rendezvous position with SLAM.

"I don't like it," the pilot declared to the copilot who was seated beside him in the cockpit area. "You see the strobe anywhere?"

"Negative," returned the copilot.

His voice was tense, and both of them found it impossible to shake off the disquieting feeling that the situation on the ground had gone bad.

The pilot hovered the Pave Low over the designated LZ while the door gunners behind their GE Miniguns searched the ground below through the glowing green view field of their night-vision goggles.

Their practiced eyes were alert, sensitive to any movement indicating human presence on the ground below.

But although the Pave Low chopper and her crew hovered over the jungle clearing for several minutes, in direct contradiction of their orders not to linger over the RV site and to return immediately to base if the operatives were not on-site, they could see no sign of the commando force they had inserted two days before.

"What do we do?" asked the copilot, vainly searching the ground through the big chopper's cockpit canopy, yet still seeing nothing as he strained his eyes to see.

"We can't stay here anymore," the pilot answered, his face a grim mask betraying the inner turmoil he felt. "We've already stayed too long. I'm taking her back."

The Pave Low ascended straight up into the black night sky as the pilot manipulated the cyclic pitch stick and collective, feeding more torque to the hungry rotors.

The pilot didn't break radio silence to communicate with the Navy frigate *Fort Worth* in the Gulf of Thailand, which was their destination.

Nor did any of the men on board speak for long moments after the rotorcraft swung south across the jungle canopy of southern Thailand.

The throbbing of the Pave Low's engines as it left the RV miles behind was the only sound that broke the stillness of the night.

DEAL SLATER was taking fire from the attackers below. As he ran through the jungle, he stopped to set booby traps in his wake. These were intended to slow down his pursuers, disorient them and whittle down their numbers, making them pay big for every foot of earth they covered.

Now, as he paused to catch his breath beside a wide-trunked jungle tree, Slater unshipped a frag grenade from his load-bearing suspenders.

Looping a length of parachute cord to the cotter pin which secured the spoon to the fuze of the antipersonnel submunition, Slater taped the grenade to the base of the tree trunk and ran the thin green milspec cord across the ground below the leaf litter, almost completely concealing it.

Raised a quarter-inch above the jungle floor, the trip wire would be invisible until stumbled upon. If the troops were careful, they would avoid tripping it.

But Slater had killed several of his pursuers already, and the nonprofessional paramilitary force would almost certainly be spooked and angered and thrown off balance by the tactics he'd used against them.

Their emotions would be guiding them now instead of their intelligence, and that was always a fatal mistake in the combat zone.

Now Slater moved stealthily from his position and repeated the same procedure some ten meters ahead.

Taking the GPS unit from its pouch on his suspenders, Slater consulted the Magellan and set his course toward the team's rally point.

Acting quickly, he reached the high ground just ahead and hunched down into a profile-degrading position of concealment where he could observe the trap he'd set.

A few moments later the first of the group of soldiers tripped the hidden cord and detonated the grenade, blowing apart one of their members in a burst of jagged shrapnel and concussive blast effect.

Stepping around the remains of their comrade, they tripped the second trap, severely wounding another man, who let out an agonizing scream as he was caught in the fragmentation zone of the unexpected burst. As he lay screaming and moaning, Slater hurled two more frag grenades into the center of the mass of disorientated men.

He had waited two seconds before making the toss so that the grenades would detonate as airbursts, significantly increasing the intensity of the blast they generated.

The grenades detonated with two loud *crumps* and two more soldiers were down, mortally wounded.

Only a few more unfriendlies remained alive on the ground, and Slater decided to goad the survivors into a charge where they would be exposed to his fire. The Spectre did not have the range or stopping power of the Krinovs and Kalashnikovs that the paramilitaries ported, but its high-capacity magazine gave Slater the ability to pour sustained fire on the stragglers.

This, added to the fact that the enemy were enraged and frightened to the point of acting without thinking, made the strategy a sound bet with a potentially high payoff.

Triggering a few quick bursts of PB fire, Slater received wild answering fire in return.

"Come on, you bastard sons of whores!" he shouted down from above, the jungle acoustics making his voice float eerily. "Try and kill me! If you don't, I will hunt all of you down and make widows of your wives and orphans of your children!"

The words were calculated to whip his antagonists to a blind fury, and Slater knew that the chances of his English being understood were better than even.

"Fuck you!" came the shouted reply less than a minute later, confirming that Slater had been clearly understood.

The defiant shout came almost simultaneously with the forward rush of the three remaining men toward his position.

Firing their autorifles as they ran toward Slater, the men shouted curses at the American commando, no longer functioning as a cohesive unit but each acting as an individual trying to settle his own score with the taunting man.

But Slater had already moved to another position, and he opened up on them when they were well within range of the Spectre's fire.

Death to his quarry was as swift as it was unexpected by them. The group of Shan United paramilitaries were turning into his line of fire as the first of the 9 mm bullets fired by the fast-rotoring Spectre whizzed through the air.

In the split second available to them, they tried to bring their weapons into position, but their fire was wild as Slater continued to pour burst after burst into the trio.

It was all over for the kills, though.

Under the impacting steeljackets, the movement of the targets was jerky and uncontrolled. One fired a burst at the ground before collapsing sideways, another flung out his arms as he tumbled to the ground, and the third seemed to attempt a half leap before toppling straight onto his face and lying motionless with blood pumping from the huge rip in the side of his throat.

Establishing that there were no more pursuers in the area, Slater reloaded his Spectre and hustled toward the strike team's rally point, hoping against hope that the other two SLAM commandos, who were taking their chances against superior odds, had been also successful in their bid to make the RV.

19

Slater had spent an hour watching from the concealment of the dense jungle bush at the team's rally
point. When he first detected the gentle rustling of
vegetation on the fringes of the small clearing, he
aimed his Spectre SMG. He relaxed when at last he
saw the familiar shock of blond hair belonging to
Mason Hawke.

Following close behind Hawke was Eddie Bishop.
He had reached the rally point by means of an alter-
nate route that closely paralleled the one which Slater
himself had taken.

Soon the three SLAM strikers were working toward a consensus on how to proceed in the aftermath of the missed chopper RV and the shock
assaults by jungle paramilitaries.

Hawke related to his teammates that he had been
forced to use the booby-trapped commo equipment
that the team carried on the strike as bait to lure his
pursuers into a kill trap. The trap had successfully
taken out the Shan United paramilitaries, although
in doing so the specialized field equipment had been
forfeited.

This meant that both the burst transmitter and the satellite-uplinked frequency-hopping radio by which they could transmit directly to the Navy frigate *Fort Worth* were no longer available to them.

Getting out military sector maps compiled from satellite phototelemetry and recently updated, as well as their hand-held Magellan global positioning system units, they proceeded to brainstorm a fallback option.

The maps showed clearly that the dense jungle and mountain country in which they found themselves made their chances of walking out nearly nonexistent.

With the amount of manpower available to Kuhn Sa, the three-man team would be eventually overwhelmed by sheer force of numbers alone. Even now more troops were probably being pumped into the area to saturate it, and eventually they would be caught in an ever-tightening ring.

The drug warlord was playing for keeps, and there was no getting around the fact that SLAM was playing its deadly game of hide-and-seek on Kuhn Sa's home turf.

Slater discovered what he thought might prove a gambit worth taking and called this to the attention of his men. His finger circled an area on the sector map that was located only a few kilometers from their present position at the rally point.

"If we can reach the chopper compound indicated here," Slater said to Hawke and Bishop, "then we're maybe looking at the possibility of flying out."

"Chancy," Bishop put in. "There's no guarantee that any of the aircraft are in operational condition."

The helicopter compounds dotting the jungles of Thailand, Laos and Vietnam were relics of the war in Vietnam. Superannuated Huey slicks, or gunships stripped of their weapons and turned into slicks, were presently kept in service and used for local shuttle runs.

"You got any better ideas?" Hawke asked.

"Fresh out," Bishop returned, not smiling.

"Let's get moving," Slater said, already punching up the coordinates of the chopper compound on his Magellan and hefting his rucksack onto his back, suddenly feeling the fatigue brought on by the hammering stress of the past dozen hours that made his legs ache from swollen muscles and punished ligaments.

It was already well past daybreak, and Slater would have preferred to wait until darkness to move out, if for no other reason than to permit the team to take a much-needed rest break. The tactical situation made this option a nonstarter, however.

Mobility and surprise would be their best assets in their bid to reach safety. Mobility, surprise and plenty of luck.

HAWKE TOOK THE POINT again, and Slater and Bishop orbited on the rear flanks of the patrol formation as the strike team began to mobilize through the jungle toward their objective.

Because they were humping the bush during daylight conditions, their visibility to spotters was enhanced.

Owing to this fact, SLAM negotiated the mountainous jungle terrain slowly and cautiously, doubling back and breaking sideways at intervals in an effort to evade detection and determine the presence of pursuit forces in the zone of operations.

Throughout these maneuvers, the strike team was steadily and progressively working its way along a northeasterly course toward the position marked on the map.

It was already well into the afternoon of SLAM's third day in-country when Slater and Bishop heard the two clicks in their commo headsets informing them that Hawke, who was some twenty meters ahead of them, had gotten a visual confirm on the location of the chopper compound they were heading for.

As Hawke leaned against the wide trunk of a tall jungle tree, he saw Slater and Bishop move cautiously through the undergrowth toward his position. Once they'd linked up, the three commandos conducted a preliminary area recon.

The chopper compound did indeed appear to be fully operational. There were two Huey slicks in evidence, both of Vietnam-era vintage from the looks of them.

One of the choppers, in close proximity to what appeared to be a maintenance shed, was probably down for servicing. Its engine cowl was pulled up to expose the wires, tubing and machinery within.

The other Huey in the compound looked as if it might be in flying condition, though.

This chopper sat on the ground and was situated a few meters from a circular hut with an angled tin roof built on stilts. The rising heat of the day was already evident from the lines of thermal distortion rising from its fuselage.

A poorly maintained fence constructed of barbed wire strung from wooden stakes hammered into the ground formed a perimeter fence around the compound, one that was by no means secure.

At first there didn't appear to be any sign of human activity, but as the commandos continued to take stock of the situation, they saw two men in civilian clothes exit the tin-roofed hut and walk toward the chopper sitting on the ground.

One of the men wore grease-stained mechanic's overalls, while the other one wore a T-shirt and jeans. There was a brief exchange of conversation between them, whereupon the mechanic hooked up an APU to the Huey and turned it on, filling the silence with the throbbing of a motor as the unit fed power to the engines.

The man in the jeans then climbed into the cockpit of the chopper while the mechanic went into the shed where the other slick was down for servicing, and he shut the cockpit door with a crack that echoed through the lazy stillness of the sun-drenched late morning.

"Looks promising," Bishop put in from his concealed vantage point in the jungle tree line beyond the compound's perimeter. It was apparent that they had arrived just as one of the compound's two choppers was being primed for takeoff.

The team checked their weapons, loading fresh magazines into the Barret H-Bars, the single Spectre SMG and SIG 9 mm sidearms and then prepared to move on its strike objective.

The target was soft, and the two men in the vicinity were unarmed and could be easily disabled. It looked like a cakewalk. But just before SLAM moved to take the position, an unforeseen development occurred.

"Damn," Slater cursed. "I knew it looked too easy."

The deuce-and-a-half rumbled suddenly from out of the jungle, stopping short of the compound's gate with a screech of worn brake shoes as the driver honked his horn.

Hearing the blaring beyond the compound's fence, the mechanic emerged from the maintenance shed and, after an exchange of words, opened the gate to permit the truck to enter.

Once inside the compound, the squad of armed troops jumped from the transport truck and deployed through the area under the command of one of the men who had ridden in the cab.

Slater, Hawke and Bishop exchanged glances, all of them crunching the numbers in their heads. The bottom line was immediately clear to them. They could either strike fast and hard and attempt to take the compound the hard way or stand pat.

"Let's go," Slater said, unsafing his weapon and setting it on full-auto fire.

20

The path of the raw-steel charge took advantage of a section of perimeter fence that had apparently fallen down and had not been repaired. The strands of rusted barbed wire actually lay buried part way in the weedy ground overgrown with chest-high, blue-flowered *ya farang* grass.

With the .50-caliber Barret machine gun in Bishop's tactical-gloved hands providing suppressing fire, Slater and Hawke unshipped frag and APERS grenades from their load bearing suspenders and tossed them at their targets.

The grenades fragmented as airbursts, their splinter radius and blast effect enhanced due to the absence of ground absorption.

Several of the O.D.-fatigued troops were killed or wounded by the combined effect of autofire from the blazing MG and razoring shrapnel from the grenade bursts in the initial seconds of the assault.

Before the shocked troopers could orient themselves, the Spectre SMG in Slater's hands and the other .50-caliber SAW wielded by Mason Hawke were both cycling furiously.

Arcing tracers went streaking across the compound as they walked their low-trajectory fire, steamrollering their surprised targets and adding more kills to the fast-rising body count as Bishop moved in with his weapon flaming at his hip.

Fanning out as they breached the compound perimeter, each SLAM striker picked his target and moved in to kill it, taking care to avoid damaging the Huey chopper, which the team hoped would be their ticket out of the Shan hellzone.

Slater homed in on two of the Shan United troopers who were attempting to make a getaway in the six-wheeled transport truck.

One paramilitary was already behind the steering wheel, while another man propped the barrel of a Krinov assault weapon on the frame of the rolled-down window on the opposite side of the cab and threw bursts of autofire at anything that moved, sliding the barrel from side to side.

A burst from Slater's Spectre punched through the cab door, stitching the shooter across his midsection before he'd cooked off a third of his clip. The AKR dropped from his nerveless fingers as he sagged forward against the dashboard.

Slater sprinted for the cab of the deuce-and-a-half, already pulling a minigrenade from his load-bearing suspenders.

Reaching the cab, he tossed in the grenade and quickly dodged sideways, hearing the muffled report as the grenade went off in the enclosed space a pulse beat later.

Flames belched and smoke billowed from the truck's shattered window frames, and Slater heard the sound of screaming from inside the cab. Seeing that the driver was not yet dead, Slater pulled a second minigrenade from his suspenders and tossed it into the cab, too, finishing the job with another dose of shrapnel and blast.

Hawke and Bishop were meanwhile taking fire as Slater moved toward the cockpit of the Huey chopper, where the pilot was likewise trying to stage a getaway of his own.

The Huey's rotors were already spinning, though not yet fast enough to dish, but in imminent danger of doing so.

Reaching the aircraft, Slater hopped onto the nearest of the helo's skids and tugged at the door latch.

Predictably the cockpit door was locked.

Panicked, the pilot pulled up on the collective pitch stick, pushed the cyclic forward and increased the revolutions of the rotors spinning overhead. Slater could now feel the slight yawing of the chopper as it rose like a ponderous creature shaking off a deep sleep.

Moving quickly, Slater let the Spectre ride its elastic combat sling and hoisted himself up from the running board into the open side hatch of the rising slick.

Once inside the slick's cabin, Slater fisted the Spectre SMG and ordered the pilot to set the slick back down on the landing site.

The pilot's response was to pull a small black handgun from a chest rig, twist around in his seat and squeeze off a round of .45 ACP steel at Slater.

This move was not tactically sound with a gun already pointing at him. Slater immediately triggered off a PB burst, deliberately aiming high to decrease the risk of striking any critical instrumentation on the Huey's panel.

Striking its target, the burst of 9 mm Spectre bullets sheared away most of the rear of the pilot's skull in a red cloud of shattered bone and pulped brain tissue.

Still secured by its harness to the seat, the pilot's body writhed and thrashed around in a last nervous-system response as blood sprayed from the raggedly severed carotids. But his grip on the collective pitch stick at last relaxed in death, and the rotorcraft was unsteadily dropping back to earth.

Had the Huey been more than a foot or two off the ground when the firefight took place, the results might have been disastrous. But the chopper merely lurched back to earth and settled on its skids with its rotors slowing after a rocky touchdown.

Unstrapping the corpse and pushing it out the side door onto the ground, Slater checked the blood-spattered instrument panels of the again stationary Huey slick.

All indicators appeared normal, and except for the windshield shattered by two bullets from the multi-round burst, the chopper seemed unharmed.

Moving back into the cabin, Slater looked out through one of the open side hatches.

The chattering of automatic-weapons fire was still continuing sporadically as he took stock of the hot zone. Hawke and Bishop, he could see, were answering small-arms fire coming from the hut and the maintenance shed, where some of the troops had taken cover and could not be dislodged.

"Two and Three, over to the chopper on the double," Slater said into the rice-grain mike of his AN/PRC comset. "Bird is secure. Repeat, bird is secure."

"That's a roger," Slater heard the no-sweat tones of Hawke's voice say as he simultaneously saw the two commandos back toward his position. Their long-barreled black Barret MGs were belching fire and lead at the entrenched shooters as they staged a fighting retreat toward the waiting helicopter.

Dropping down and setting his weapon on 3-round burstfire, Slater added the 9 mm rounds of the Spectre SMG to the .50-caliber machine gun fire cranked out by Bishop and Hawke, who by now had almost reached the Huey's tail rotor boom.

Yelling for Hawke to get inside and get the chopper moving, Slater took over Hawke's squad auto weapon as he leaned out the hatch of the slick and rotored suppressing fire at the hot points of cycling flame from the structures where the holdouts were located.

Bullets thunked into the hull of the aircraft, augering through the thinly armored bulkheads and ricocheting off the floor. Bishop crouched in the opposite hatchway and added the thunder of his own .50-caliber gun to the earsplitting bolt clatter of Slater's brass-spitting weapon.

Together they sent zigzagging streams of glowing tracers into the enemy fire positions as Hawke, behind the Huey's controls, pulled up on the collective and eased forward the cyclic pitch controls to get them airborne in a hurry.

Moments later the veteran Huey chopper was rising jerkily off the ground in the most critical seconds of lift-off before achieving the transitional lift stage, when its weight was offset by its upward velocity and it could swiftly move from the area.

Seeing that the chopper was about to take off and determined to stop it from leaving the compound, the holed-up troops moved out into the open from their positions.

Already more than six feet off the ground now, the Huey lurched sideways as Hawke fed more torque to the hungrily spinning rotor on top of the cabin.

Staccato bursts of autofire continued to punch through the chopper's hull, leaving petaled holes to mark the bullets' passage while Slater and Bishop angled their guns downward to sight in on the Shan troopers firing their heavy-caliber AK weapons from the ground below.

Scoring successive hits, Slater and Bishop saw three of the troopers go down as they achieved transitional lift and then rose sharply upward with the speed of an express elevator.

Within seconds the chopper had ascended to a cruising altitude of some sixty feet, bringing the rotorcraft just out of range of the chugging fire coming from the small arms of the hostiles on the ground, who were not letting up in their futile bid to sink the slick.

As the hollow chatter of automatic gunfire from below began to fade into the echoing distance, Hawke swung the chopper around on a course heading that would take its occupants across the southern tier of Thailand and back to the frigate.

In time he would use the chopper's radio to send a Mayday message. But they were out of the firezone now, out of danger. And each of the three clandestine warriors needed a little time to get their pulse rates back to something resembling normal.

PART THREE:

Zero In

21

Disgraced by failure, General Dao had only one recourse: to accept the sentence of death.

The man who had given his assurance to Kuhn Sa that the commando force that had spread carnage throughout the druglord's well-ordered jungle empire would be destroyed had not kept his word. But his date with the executioner would come off as scheduled.

In the jungle encampment, hundreds of Shan Army regulars formed a circle where the execution of the disgraced warrior was to take place. All of them would bear witness to the heavy, final reckoning of one who had betrayed their leader and their cause, who had lost face and been tainted beyond salvage by his failure.

"Here before you is a worthless dog who has caused the death of our comrades by his ineptitude," declared the hooded executioner who approached Dao. The former general, now stripped naked, was tied to a wooden cross that had been pounded securely into the center of the grassy circle. "Now he will pay the bitter price of failure."

Saying this, the executioner swung the machete in his hand and chopped off one of Dao's hands at the wrist in a single quick motion. Dao screamed in agony, his mouth open, his head thrashing as blood pumped from his severed wrist.

The executioner looked to Kuhn Sa, who raised his hand high to indicate for him to proceed with his brutal work. Again the executioner wielded his sharply honed blade and hacked off the general's other hand. He then chopped Dao's legs off at the knees in a series of equally swift and deft motions.

"Kill him!" someone yelled from within the assembled ranks of the Shan United Army troops. "Kill the treacherous dog!"

Others among the encircling spectators picked up the chant that called for the general's blood to be spilled on the ground.

In a matter of minutes, the throng of Shan Army troopers was howling for the final punishment to be exacted from Dao. They had been whipped to a frenzy and now, eyes bright, hands raised with bunched fists, they called down the ultimate punishment on his head.

Kuhn Sa stood up and raised his hand, a sign for the crowd to fall silent. This it immediately did, and in the stillness that held sway in the moments following, Kuhn Sa turned to the executioner, made a fist and brought his arm down sharply, giving the executioner permission to deliver the coup de grace to his mortally wounded victim.

Bowing low, the executioner rose to grip the machete in both hands. Raising it above his head, he brought it down with tremendous force and severed Dao's head in one swift chop that sliced through the neck vertebrae securing it to the spinal column.

The decapitated head dropped to the ground and rolled for a distance, the blood dripping from it becoming caked with dust and bits of grass and twigs.

The executioner walked forward and picked up the head of Dao by the lank black hair. Holding his hand aloft, he shook the hideous remains mockingly and walked around in a circle to show the watching ranks what the final humiliation of Dao looked like, how a human being could be brought lower than dung with a few quick strokes of a well-sharpened cutting implement.

All of the assembled ranks knew that this was as much a warning to them as a retribution to Dao. Kuhn Sa's message had gotten across in graphic terms that could not be misunderstood by any single man among the Shan United troops. Its meaning was clear to every man: to lose face before Kuhn Sa was to lose one's very life.

At a signal from Kuhn Sa, the executioner tossed the head to the ground and walked through the ranks and disappeared from the circle of death, leaving the mutilated corpse sagging in its restraints above a pool of blood.

Kuhn Sa again rose and addressed the assemblage before dismissing them.

"Look well and long upon what has happened to this disgraced one," he shouted at the hundreds of onlookers who formed an olive-drab-colored sea, his voice carrying on the wind to be heard all the way at the rear of the assembled ranks. "Dedicate yourselves to success, or such a fate may well be yours."

As the crowd dissipated, Kuhn Sa watched them melt away into the surrounding huts. He smiled inwardly, although his countenance wore his characteristic blank expression. He had accomplished much, he thought, and with little effort expended to achieve his desired ends.

Not only had he delivered an object lesson to his troops, but by amply demonstrating the ruthlessness to which he was capable of resorting, he had also showed any of his subordinates who might have entertained ideas of capitalizing on his failure to suppress or neutralize the commando raiders that Kuhn Sa was still strong, still vicious and, above all else, still very much in control.

But Kuhn Sa entertained no illusions about how long such an example would serve to deter attempts at toppling him from his position as maximum leader of the Shan United Army if he did not actually put an end to the commando strikes before too long.

If he failed to stem them, no further displays of strength or ruthlessness would cancel out the impression among his troops that he had become too weak to hold the reins of power, and his own death would swiftly follow.

As intelligent as he was tenacious, Kuhn Sa believed he had found a way out of his predicament, however.

His informants were many and they stretched as far as Washington, D.C., into the very halls of the American Congress itself. Kuhn Sa's trusted information had it that a future strike against his Shan stronghold was likely.

If such an assault did in fact come about, then he would be ready to turn the game around on his adversaries. If no further assaults were initiated, then he would have time to consolidate his forces, rebuild his strength in the field, increase his output of the opium poppy.

No matter what the outcome, Kuhn Sa would be ready.

Kuhn Sa would win, as he always did.

WHILE ON A WORKING vacation at his retreat in Big Sur, California, the President of the United States engaged in a series of staff meetings with his national-security adviser, the director of central intelligence and other high-echelon personnel.

The subject of these meetings was a potential follow-on strike in the aftermath of the tremendous damage that the covert team inserted into Kuhn Sa's territory had inflicted on two important drug-processing sites.

The fact that the mission had almost been aborted due to unforeseen difficulties encountered in the field did not have any bearing on a future strike. To the President's mind, results were the only things that mattered, and in the case of these paramilitary efforts, the results had been far better than anticipated.

Photo reconnaissance by Keyhole satellites had demonstrated these facts with crystal clarity.

The finished Intelligence prepared by analysts at the CIA's national photographic interpretation center showed graphically the extent of the damage inflicted on the covert jungle processing center and the airstrip by the SLAM team.

The damage to the target was so extensive that the President, who sometimes needed to have what he was looking at clarified by his Intelligence and national-security experts, had no difficulty whatsoever in assessing the nature and ramifications of the strikes.

The vicinity of the temple, which he understood to be the initial target, was marked in a several meter radius by the telltale blackening of recent explosions.

So good was the resolution of the Keyhole photo Intelligence, even from an altitude of better than 150,000 feet, that the President could also clearly distinguish the bodies—and in some cases the body parts—of hostile troops scattered across the strike zone.

At the second site surgically hit by the SLAM team, the damage was every bit as extensive. The transshipment site had been completely burned to the ground, and the number of dead Shan United regulars was impressive.

"This looks darned good," the President said after asking a few perfunctory questions of his advisers. "I want the pace stepped up," he went on. "I want another strike to commence as soon as possible."

Having said that, the President indicated his wish to get started soon on the next business of the morning.

22

A few weeks after the second deep-strike operation, which had almost ended in debacle, SLAM was informed that the team was again being tasked with a third strike on Kuhn Sa's jungle realm.

This strike was to be even more ambitious than the two that had preceded it.

They would be moving against Kuhn Sa's main base of operations, located deep in the most inaccessible part of the Shan.

As had been the case with the destruction of the fortresslike estate of Kuhn Sa's chief druglord, Yuen Tat Chow, an air strike would be called in to destroy the vital infrastructure and chief material assets of Kuhn Sa's drug empire.

This time the object of the strike would be a major poppy-growing area where the crop was ripening and ready to yield a bumper harvest of opium poppies.

Slater, Hawke and Bishop rode the Pave Low chopper into the skies from their dustoff point on the aft deck of the Navy frigate secured for their covert strike under the multinational and interagency

ADNET—antidrug network—communications and Intelligence program, which provided for the sharing of manpower and resources in the war against drugs.

The Pave Low chugged over the treetops on its low-trajectory flight path toward the strike team's insertion point, deep within the mountain country of the Shan range.

Once down on the ground, NVGs were unshipped, donned and initialized in a routine that had become second nature from the two strikes that had preceded this new covert offensive.

The strike team melted into the jungle as the Pave Low lifted off and ascended into the sky, embarking on the return leg of its journey toward its covert base. SLAM was about to embark on its incursion into the heart and soul of the drug warlord's activities to slice away a growing cancer with the mercilessness of a surgeon's blade.

WITH THE MISSION CLOCK ticking, SLAM steamrollered along on its predetermined course toward the heart of the Shan, into the dark center of Kuhn Sa's base of operations.

Once there, they would illuminate the target and call in a covert air strike as they had done on their initial foray into Mae Sai.

This time, though, the warheads of the air-to-ground munitions would contain a mix of napalm and recently developed chemical defoliants based on natural plant growth hormones that, unlike Agent Orange, were harmless to human and animal life.

This powerful amalgamation of chemicals and fire would render the poppy crop useless, resulting in the potential destruction of billions of dollars in assets.

Politically it was hoped that this action would succeed in driving the final wedge between Kuhn Sa and his allies. The desired end result of this scenario would be the overthrow of the drug warlord.

When this stage was reached, a process of political intervention would take place. After the sword of war fell, the olive branch of peace would be held out by the President's envoys.

Renewed offers of financial aid to the devastated mountain area would be made in return for a pledge to cease growing poppies and agree to a United Nations–mandated program of crop rotation.

The Intelligence analysts in Washington and Langley had decided that the psychological moment might be right and the plan could enjoy success.

But for the line forces on the ground, the theoretical abstractions of international politics and covert Intelligence were the furthest thing from their minds.

Now, hours into the mission, the shadow warriors of SLAM were humping the bush with the care of men who realize that they might have gone to the well once too often.

The first strike had punished the enemy but had also alerted him to the danger that he faced. The second strike had seen SLAM confronting an angered enemy who had nearly succeeded in preventing the team's extraction from a hot zone.

Now Slater, Hawke and Bishop were aware that they would be facing an enemy both angry and alert, a many-footed beast twice stung by the SLAM scorpion and determined not to be stung another time.

Additionally it would be an enemy which had been schooled the hard and dirty way in the weapons and tactics of the strike commandos and who would have a renewed sense of mission in stopping them once and for all.

With these factors borne in mind, as well as the negative consequences that they might engender, the SLAM team proceeded using all the precautions of jungle craft in reaching their assigned objective.

Proceeding in their triangle formation with Slater on point and Hawke and Bishop orbiting out on the flanks to the rear of the patrol, the strike team regularly swung away from the trail they followed to check for pursuit teams, then deployed to rally points from where they moved out again, taking a zigzag route toward their objective.

Their progress was unimpeded throughout the course of the night, until their movement following a stop at their third rally point. In a clearing less than a kilometer up the trail they were following, signs of activity were detected at long range.

"Check it out," Slater ordered Bishop in a low whisper.

"Good to go," came Bishop's answer.

He and Hawke covered Bishop as he stole up on what turned out to be an encampment in the jungle, where a group of men huddled around a cooking fire.

After a few minutes of covert observation, Bishop determined that the men were not Shan Army forces, nor even Chiu Chow, the Asian equivalent of La Cosa Nostra soldiers, but something on a lower echelon than either category.

"I make them itinerant smugglers," he said. "They're probably either on their way to or from Kuhn Sa's base."

It was decided that the smugglers—if that is what they turned out to be—should be interrogated to provide Intelligence on the whereabouts of Kuhn Sa's base.

Each member of the strike team was aware that this would also entail disposing of the smugglers, who could not be allowed to leave the area alive.

Though hoping this final turn of events would not prove necessary, each also knew that they would have to be prepared to take them down if necessary.

A few minutes later the group of men were surprised by the sudden appearance of armed men who suddenly moved from the jungle into the firelit encampment in the clearing.

One of them stood, swinging an AKM into position, but was smart enough not to complete the arc when he saw that Bishop already had the drop on him. The man flung the weapon to the ground and

held up his hands in a universal gesture of uncondi-
tional surrender.

Slater stepped into the clearing, regarding the men
up close and not liking what he saw in their eyes and
faces. They had the look of cutthroats and thieves.

While Hawke covered them with silenced SMGs
carried on the mission, Bishop was searching the
contents of the packs they had been carrying.

"Take a look at this," he said, gesturing to Slater.

When Slater did, he discovered that the packs
contained an assortment of goods, including quantities of processed heroin. These men were smugglers but also drug mules, as well, making a run
down toward the coast along an opium-smuggling
trail.

Slater's command of Thai was limited but it was
good enough for him to establish that the smugglers
had left Kuhn Sa's encampment the day before and
were on their way across the border into neighbor-
ing Laos.

They told Slater further that the encampment lay
just over the next jungle ridge line, about a day's
journey on foot from their present position, which
jibed with the latest satellite-generated Intelligence
SLAM had on the position of their mission objective.

Having been apprised of these facts, Slater as team
commander grappled with the question of what to do
next, how to decide the fate of the men.

Kuhn Sa would pay a great price for any information about those who had dealt him such painful blows, and Slater had no illusions that the smugglers, in return for their lives, would withhold from informing on them if they were able to do so.

The men in the clearing were obviously scared, and Slater was considering whether to issue them a warning and leave it at that as he scanned their mute faces.

But one of them decided the issue for the entire group by taking action when standing pat would have proved the more viable option.

The smuggler had been inching his hand onto the butt of the semiautomatic pistol holstered beneath his shirt and now quickly brought it out. A burst from Bishop's gun knocked him flat onto his back with several rounds lodged in his upper torso.

Scrambling for weapons of their own, the others made a quick transition from victims to armed and dangerous threats.

More silenced autobursts from Bishop and Hawke summarily put away the other members of the group. It was all over in a few seconds, the spasm of violence having claimed the lives of all the smugglers in the clearing.

"Sanitize the area," Slater ordered after the final bursts were fired.

They worked together, breaking out entrenching tools and digging graves in which to bury the dead and their illicit cargo.

In order to keep jungle scavengers away from the site, the team poured CN gas powder, brought along expressly for that purpose, into the holes before covering them up with earth again.

After the graves were covered over with earth, they placed underbrush over the sites to complete the task of concealing the kills.

Again donning their night-observation goggles, the strike team moved on toward their principal mission objective.

They didn't realize that their presence in the area had been compromised by concealed spotters deliberately placed in their line of march, spotters linked by radio to Kuhn Sa.

23

The hill tribe's village was situated less than twenty klicks along SLAM's line of march. Even from a good distance away, the Montagnard village appeared to be deserted.

Slater went in close to reconnoiter while Hawke and Bishop kept the perimeter under close cover in the jungle just beyond it.

Before he had gone very far, he found the first of several corpses of the Meo tribesmen who had inhabited the village. Multiple entry wounds on the corpses attributable to automatic-weapons fire made it apparent that armed action had been responsible for the deaths.

Wary of concealed booby traps, Slater made certain not to touch the bodies before continuing his recon.

His weapon unsafed and held ready for instant deployment, Slater probed cautiously, proceeding through the village at a slow, deliberate pace.

As he moved from the initial kills encountered, the SLAM strike leader scanned the ground for concealed trip wires that might be tethered to munitions or the camouflaged trigger lines of jungle mantraps that might have been left behind by whoever had been responsible for the carnage.

"Three to One. Say your situation," he heard Bishop inquire via the earbud of his AN/PRC comset.

"Signs of recent hostilities," Slater replied, his eyes on the ground as he stepped carefully over a transparent nylon line strung across his path. "Just encountered a booby trap. Wait one."

"Roger," Bishop replied.

Crouching low on his haunches, Slater ran his eye along the wire and found its terminus. This was a grenade cluster concealed just beneath the lip of the village well.

Sliding his Ka-bar combat knife from its boot scabbard, Slater carefully cut the trigger cord and disarmed the crude but effective booby trap. He placed the grenades into his rucksack for possible recycling.

Then, reaching into a camo-pattern nylon pouch on his load-bearing suspenders, he removed a Cyalume light-stick. The transparent plastic tube containing the chemical mixture was marked to indicate that it was rated at a one-hour life span.

Crimping the transparent plastic cylinder filled with a luminescing chemical mixture between his fingers, he shook the Cyalume to mix the chemicals and cause it to give off a bright green light.

"Disarmed the booby trap," he said into the rice-grain mike at his lips, then he dropped the light-stick beside the well. "Am marking my path. Proceeding with probe."

"Affirmative," Bishop said back over the head-set earpiece.

Porting his Spectre, Slater moved from the well toward the first of the handful of thatched bamboo huts that comprised the structures of the mountain hamlet.

He checked out the largest and closest of the huts first. Its bamboo door was ajar. Owing to the possibility of a concealed booby trap, Slater proceeded in his next movements with deliberate caution.

Positioning himself at the side of the doorway nearest to the rusty hinges of the partially open door, Slater nudged it open, using the barrel of the sound-suppressor equipped Spectre SMG.

The door swung open without incident.

With the Spectre extended at chest level, Slater swept into the hut on a low crouch, breaking sideways as he entered the dwelling.

Inside the Meo hut he discovered some signs of recent habitation although no villagers were in evidence, either alive or dead.

On the hearth, set on a blackened metal grille sitting atop a jumble of stones, were a cluster of utensils containing a half-cooked meal of fish sauce and rice. The stones of the cooking hearth were still warm to the touch.

"This hut is secure," Slater said into his AN/PRC portable commo unit. "Proceeding with probe."

"Affirmative," Bishop said back.

After he withdrew from the hut, the largest one in the place, Slater probed the one beside it, dropping more light-sticks to mark his path as he continued the recon.

Here, too, there were signs of recent habitation and hasty departure, although he did find the body of an old Meo woman and a young boy inside, riddled with bullet wounds.

Continuing on his probe of the village, Slater checked out the remaining huts.

One other dwelling contained more recently shot victims and all were devoid of living human beings. Stepping from the final hut, Slater issued his final status report to his men waiting in the bush beyond the village perimeter.

"The village's secure," he said, adding instructions for Hawke and Bishop to link up with him at the well and to take care to follow the trail of light-sticks he'd laid down to avoid setting off any booby traps he might have missed.

The village lay across their line of march, and cutting through it would be faster than going around it.

Minutes later Hawke and Bishop had joined Slater in the hamlet. Ordering a rest break, they conferred regarding the possible reasons for the carnage they had encountered here.

The prevailing theory was that Kuhn Sa had visited retribution on the hill people for some infraction. Even a petty crime could be repaid with massive reprisals in the drug warlord's savage domain. The world controlled by Kuhn Sa was one in which far more ancient codes of law than those normally understood by Americans were in force.

SLAM lingered in the mountain hamlet for several minutes before moving out. And then, just as they were preparing to hump the bush again, the stuttering of automatic-weapons fire broke the deceptive stillness of the mountains.

Without warning, the team was taking fire.

Slater felt the lancinating pain in his leg even as he dived for the cover of the well while to his left and right, Hawke and Bishop were both breaking for cover inside the doorway of the peasant hut just behind them.

As multiple impacting bullets sent clods of earth flying all around them, the strike team oriented itself to the new threat, crunching the numbers that would give them the odds against survival.

"I'm hit," Slater transmitted as he sighted the Spectre and fired into the line of muzzle-flashes coming from the crouched shapes of camo-fatigued paramilitary troops who were forming a ring around the village. "Say your status."

"Unhurt," Bishop said back.

"Same here," Hawke replied. "How bad is it?"

A brief lull came after the first spasm of attack. The SLAM team used the seconds of comparative calm to reload their weapons while Slater checked his bleeding leg wound.

He saw that he'd been luckier than he had a right to expect. The heavy-caliber AK bullet had passed through the fleshy part of his thigh and out the other end, but he was bleeding heavily.

The round had probably damaged an artery.

Getting his first-aid kit out of his rucksack, Slater applied a pressure tourniquet just above the wound after sprinkling it with sulfa powder. The bleeding began to ebb and slowly stopped entirely.

The wound had stabilized, Slater informed his men. The question of how to now proceed remained unanswered. They had stumbled into a crudely set but effective enemy ambush and were now in imminent danger of death or capture, which would probably add up to the same thing in the end.

Yet from the appearance of the opposing force, it was likely that they were looking at battalion strength, and these were numbers that SLAM had no chance of taking on and winning against despite their skills.

Slater crunched the numbers and came up with a zero-sum game every time he calculated the odds. But what he had to do was clear to him, and he knew also that he would have to act quickly in order to bring it off successfully.

"We're out of here," he said to Hawke and Bishop. "Follow the Cyalumes toward the opposite end of the village. I'll take the rear and cover your retreat."

"Wait a minute, Slater," Hawke's voice said in his earphones. "You don't think we're gonna leave you here, do you?"

The pounding of automatic-weapons fire suddenly started up again. It was seemingly coming from everywhere at once. The air was suddenly thick with buzz-sawing lead, and the noise was deafening.

"I said *move!*" Slater shouted into his mike, hefting his Spectre and returning fire. "That's an order. *Go!*"

"Affirmative," he heard Hawke say, his voice tense.

Moments later Slater heard the steady hammering of their big .50-caliber machine guns alternately punching out a deadly fire stream as they withdrew along the route of escape marked by the glowing green Cyalume light-sticks.

They moved leapfrog fashion, one covering the other as they scuttled along their line of retreat.

Slater saw uniformed men moving forward in a surge of bodies as he reloaded a fresh 50-round clip of PB ammunition into the Spectre SMG and sighted on the front of the mass through its iron sights. Triggering a burst, he cut down two men and received an intense salvo of massed automatic fire in answer.

By this time Hawke and Bishop had reached the perimeter of the village. Looking back, they could see the blazing muzzle-flashes of Slater's weapon as he fired on the advancing phalanx of O.D.-clad Shan Army regulars who, despite the casualties they were taking under fire, were penetrating the village.

"Slater, where the hell are you?" Hawke shouted into his rice-grain mike. "Move, damn it. We're covering your position!"

"Negative," Slater replied over AN/PRC commo. "Move out. Proceed to rally point Cleaver and signal Convention for extraction."

"No way, man!"

It was Bishop's voice this time, anxious and stressed to the max.

"That's a fucking order!" Slater shouted above the chattering of the enemy guns. "Get going. I can't keep them back for long."

Bishop tensed at the perimeter of the field. His eyes were focused on the troops moving toward Slater down behind the well.

Hawke, beside Bishop, saw that his partner was a pulse beat away from doing something terminally stupid such as rushing back into the white-hot center of the firezone.

"We're moving out," Hawke said into his comset while he grabbed hold of Bishop's arm. "Let's go, buddy," he continued, speaking to Bishop. "I can't let you do what you're thinking of."

"I'm going back, man!" Bishop shouted at Hawke, shrugging off his grasp.

"No way," Hawke shouted. "It's suicide."

The troops were already closing in on Slater's position. Bishop snapped out of his emotional loop and the professional soldier in him resurfaced. He knew that he couldn't go back in, not anymore.

Both SLAM commandos hustled into the bush as the enemy moved in to secure the village. The firing had stopped now, and as they entered the brush they could see Slater standing with his hands raised, under the guns of the enemy force that had taken him captive.

24

Uplinked to the orbiting communications satellite via the team's satcom radio rig, Hawke was relaying a position update to Convention via scrambled telemetry. Coded according to the NSA's unbreakable DES encryption standard, the transmission was as impervious to decryption as was possible to achieve.

The two members of the SLAM team still mobile and in the field would have preferred not to transmit at all, well aware that their report on the firefight and capture of Slater would garner an immediate order to head for the LZ and await airborne extraction.

But since no message at all from the assets deployed in the field would merely provoke a query from the mission support facility on board the Navy frigate *Fort Worth,* which would have the same end result, Hawke and Bishop decided it prudent to initiate the transmission as scheduled and take it from there.

Consulting his wrist chronometer, Hawke noted that the comsat—a Magnum-class orbital platform—would be positioned overhead in its receiving window and had begun setting up the satcom unit.

Although compact, the long-range transmitter device was made up of two separate components, the milspec hardened transceiver unit and the tripoded satellite antenna that was linked to it via a shielded coaxial cable.

When Admiral Harrington, who was personally in charge of the mission on board the frigate, came on-line, Hawke briefly and concisely reported the details of the team's firefight with Shan United Army troops and the subsequent capture of Slater by those same personnel.

"You are to make for rally point Cleaver immediately," the admiral's voice directed over the sat-com transceiver unit's headset.

"Having trouble reading you, sir," Hawke responded as he traded glances and nods with Bishop standing beside him with weapon in hand, scanning the perimeter of the temporary encampment for indications of the presence of threat. "Heavy interference," Hawke went on, continuing the charade. "Say again, sir."

The man on the other end repeated his instructions to the team in-country.

A Vietnam combat veteran himself, the admiral heard no sign of static on the line, and a shake of the head from the radio operator seated at the console beside him confirmed his suspicions that nothing of the sort was in fact happening.

The admiral had used such tactics himself in Vietnam, when as a SEAL lieutenant he chose to carry on a mission in the field despite the orders of his superiors back at base.

"Wait one, sir," Hawke said again.

He began jiggling the squelch button of the satcom transceiver in a deliberate attempt to play havoc with the communications link. "Your signal's getting weaker, sir. I think there's a problem with the rig."

"Damn it, soldier!" he heard the admiral shout in his headphones. "I'm ordering you to—"

Hawke switched off power to the unit just before the admiral could complete his sentence, which had degenerated into a series of colorful expletives.

The ploy was a transparent one, but there was no way in hell that he and Bishop were going to extract the area without at least trying to get Slater out.

They had discussed the issue of disobeying their orders, and their decision hinged on the sole question of whether or not there was any expectation of finding Slater alive.

Odds were that Slater was already bagged and tagged, both men realized, professionally and coolly assessing the situation as circumstances forced them to do.

But there would be no way to be sure beyond a reasonable doubt that their friend and commander would not remain a long-term prisoner of Kuhn Sa, a hostage to the tender mercies of the drug warlord.

If Slater had been confirmed as killed in action, that would have been one thing. But to leave him an

MIA brought forth associations in the minds of both unconventional warriors that went far beyond dedication to flag and country, military professionalism or even considerations of basic common sense.

There was an even chance that Kuhn Sa was holding Slater prisoner at his mountain encampment, possibly intending to use him as a bargaining chip in calling off the interdiction strikes that were hurting him, much as he had originally done with Victor Chin.

And it was that slim but undeniable possibility that Slater was captive and not history that sparked Bishop and Hawke's motivation to remain in the mission zone until they had gotten a confirm on Slater's whereabouts.

Before they would leave the Shan, Bishop and Hawke pledged that they would determine for themselves what his ultimate fate had been. And if they died in the attempt, that was okay, too.

BOTH MEN would have been relieved to know that Slater was in fact alive, although very much a prisoner of Kuhn Sa.

As Hawke replaced the satellite-uplinked transceiver unit into his rucksack and Bishop attended to sanitizing the temporary rest site before they broke camp, Slater was sitting under guard in the back of a canvas-covered transport truck churning its way across muddy, rutted mountain roads toward the high mountain encampment of the Shan United Army's headquarters.

Blindfolded, with his hands bound behind his back and his leg badly wounded by enemy fire, Slater was in no condition to attempt any kind of escape bid.

Deliberately exposing himself to fire during the shoot-out at the mountain hamlet, he had hoped to be killed so that he would present no threat to his men by talking under torture.

He cursed himself for having been too slow in using the lethal injector with which each team member was equipped for when capture was imminent.

Though he had pulled his SIG personal-defense weapon from its chest rig and fired point-blank at the Shan troops who had rushed him when they saw him attempting to use the lethal injector he had been equipped with, Slater had been overwhelmed by their numbers and the injector was taken from him.

Slater's options now would be limited to bearing up under torture for as long as possible, providing Hawke and Bishop with sufficient lead time to reach the rally point and extract via chopper. The longer Slater could hold out before cracking, the more vital lead time his men would have and the greater their chances of reaching safety.

If he still remained alive after that point, Slater would attempt to escape and cross the Shan into Cambodia, if possible, where the new political order displaying a cold friendliness to the United States might increase his personal chances of escape.

The journey by truck continued over the badly rutted and tortuously twisting roads for a lengthy period of time. He was being forced to sit in a cramped and uncomfortable position, and his limbs had begun to ache and his leg wound was throbbing painfully.

Slater fought against the numbing effect it had on his thinking processes. Above all else, he needed his mental faculties functioning at the highest efficiency level possible.

He knew also that in time the body's natural chemistry would produce an analgesic effect on his system, allowing him to transcend these early effects of his injuries.

For now, Slater tried to use this slack period to his best advantage. He knew that the lull he was experiencing would only be temporary; it would be the calm before the storm.

Once he reached his destination, wherever that turned out to be, it would be time to pay his dues all over again.

Casting his thoughts forward, the SLAM honcho tried to extrapolate what he might expect at the hands of his captors.

He surmised that it was likely that his destination was the Shan United Army main encampment. Kuhn Sa had demonstrated a penchant in recent months for taking hostages, and Slater felt confident that one of the commandos responsible for the covert war waged against him was a prize he would relish above all.

This seemed especially likely in consideration of all the trouble that the enemy forces had gone to in order to take him alive, when they could just as easily have killed him or allowed him to take his own life.

If this proved to be the case, then Slater could anticipate undergoing intensive, brutal interrogation, perhaps followed in time by public execution. Kuhn Sa was known to favor such tactics with captured adversaries.

The window of opportunity for an escape bid would open up during the first twenty-four to forty-eight hours after his arrival at his destination, in that event.

Slater continued to weigh his options as the excruciating pain in his leg slowly began to subside as he had expected and body chemicals released by stress and fatigue began to sharpen his mind and fill him with a raw-edged energy familiar from experience with previous wounds he had incurred in battle.

Before too long the heavy transport truck stopped with a sudden lurch, and he was pushed to his feet and shoved from the truck by the paramilitaries in whose custody he was.

Still blindfolded, Slater felt their hands clutch his bound arms as he was shoved forward, beaten and kicked by the screaming crowd through which he moved toward an unknown destination.

25

Stealthily moving through the dense jungle in the vicinity of Kuhn Sa's base, Mason Hawke and Eddie Bishop were strongly aware that they were playing a dangerous, possibly a no-win, game and that the mission clock was ticking fast on top of every other consideration.

The triple-tiered jungle was crawling with patrols, and the enemy patrols had been sent out with a single objective: to hunt them down and capture or kill them.

When Bishop caught his first glimpse of movement in the brush about twenty meters off to his right flank, Hawke was somewhere way off to his left, covering his partner's movements, mirroring Bishop's actions.

Because both commandos remained out of each other's line of sight, linked only by their radios, Bishop depressed his commo talk button twice to signal Hawke that he'd established eyeball contact with the opposition.

Selecting a spot beneath a limestone overhang, which gave him excellent concealment and from which he could still maintain a continuous watch on the patrol, Bishop waited for Hawke to join him at the hide site.

A few minutes later he detected the movement amid the darkened foliage and trained his automatic assault weapon on the BDU-garbed man-shape that approached him.

A single click on his commo unit's talk button would inform Hawke that he had reached the rally point.

"Bishop, that you?" Hawke asked, receiving the confirm and drawing near.

"Affirmative, good buddy," Bishop replied in a low whisper that carried barely at all, one of the many skills of field craft mastered over the course of rigorous training and real-world combat experience.

Now Hawke could make out Bishop's cammied-up face as he popped up from his hide site, Commando assault weapon in hand.

Moving stealthily, Hawke joined his buddy in the hole and unstrapped and pulled off his NVGs, rubbing his tired eyes, which still retained a glowing afterimage from the night-vision goggles he had been wearing throughout his night patrol.

"Do we take them or go around them?" Hawke asked Bishop after observing the hostile patrol, which was still a few-score meters from their well-concealed position.

"We don't need any shooting," Bishop returned right off. "I vote we stay here and let them pass. This is good cover, and those guys are only half-soldiers."

"I copy that," Hawke replied, nodding in assent. The troops were strictly throwaways, and if not for their numbers, even SLAM's reduced force capacity would still enable them to own the night.

Having decided on their strategy, the two covert paramilitary field assets settled down to wait out the enemy patrol.

Within a matter of minutes, the mercenaries who made up the mainstay of Kuhn Sa's Shan United troops were near enough for Hawke and Bishop to hear their voices clearly, carrying far on the cool night wind.

Unlike themselves, the Shan United paramilitaries were not in the habit of maintaining silence during field operations whenever possible and whispering when on those occasions when silence required breaking.

The SLAM commandos hadn't had the opportunity for a close-in appraisal of the enemy's tactics up until now, and what they saw came as a confirmation of their initial impressions.

These men were not professional soldiers, and their jungle craft, to coin a phrase, was more honored in the breach than the act.

To soldiers whose operational doctrine was predicated on the central fact that field craft was the single factor standing between success or failure of a mission and the life and death of the unit and its men in the field, it was astonishing that the enemy proceeded in a manner both undisciplined and inefficient.

Instead of negotiating their line of march in a patrol formation that would deploy troops at front, rear and flanks of the main squad element, the Shan Army forces were merely spread out across the jungle landscape, clustering together in small groups formed as convenience dictated.

Instead of staying alert and maintaining strict silence while they patrolled, the men were talking, joking and making enough noise to be audible across vast stretches of the jungle, where sound traveled far and enemies were afforded plenty of good concealment.

And where professional soldiers would leapfrog one another—moving from rally point to rally point in a coordinated process, as well as using sideward breaks to confuse watching adversaries—this ragtag bunch was simply beating the bush in the manner of men driving game from cover, not as military professionals stalking a dangerous and well-equipped quarry.

Against a trained opposition force, Hawke and Bishop would have taken a second look at the prospect of staying under cover until it was again clear to move out, but against these throwaways the waiting tactic was sound.

Additionally the advantage of being able to get a close-up glimpse of the Shan troops in operation instilled a renewed confidence in the hearts and minds of the two SLAM commandos.

These people were useless, Hawke and Bishop both knew. They felt a thousand percent more capable than their adversaries, and far more confident of carrying out their mission objective than they had been before taking cover.

Soon the Shan United patrol was abreast of their hide site, although apparently without having gotten any inkling that the very men whom they sought were located only a matter of inches from their position.

The patrol quickly passed by, but not until one of the Shan troops decided to relieve himself against the conveniently placed rocks of the overhang where the two SLAM commandos hunkered down, not suspecting as he watered the lush vegetation that he had almost pissed down the barrel of a gun pointed at his heart.

AFTER THE BARRACKS longhouses and the munitions shed, the commander's hut was the largest of the structures found in the compound of the base.

On the first morning of Slater's captivity, he was awakened from fitful slumbers to stare into the faces and weapons of his guards. Then they hustled him to his feet and marched him at gunpoint out of the prison hut.

The compound was already full of Shan troops, as well as their women and children. Slater felt their eyes on him, cold eyes that were full of a deep loathing.

He suspected that he had an explanation for the hate he saw directed at him.

To the Montagnard tribesmen who made up the bulk of the retainers of Kuhn Sa's drug fiefdom, the interdiction measures represented an attempt by a distant foreign power to dictate terms to them, terms that revealed little real understanding of their lives and even less interest.

To the Meo and the other tribal groupings under Kuhn Sa's protection, the druglord was a source of life and sustenance, whereas the Americans and Thai officials in Bangkok who cooperated with them were uncaring figures seeking to deprive them of the basic necessities of life.

Despite their intense hatred—one that was made clear by their shouted taunts, as well as by their cold, malicious stares as he passed them—Slater empathized with the hill people.

They had been betrayed too many times by too many causes, including the North Vietnamese and the Americans during the war in Southeast Asia.

Kuhn Sa had been the only one of their "protectors" who had delivered on his promises and who had kept his commitments to them.

It was not surprising, therefore, that they responded in kind.

But in a few minutes Slater's attention turned from the assembled ranks through which he passed to what lay ahead inside the commander's hut into which he was ushered by his armed entourage.

Pushed through the door into the humid darkness beyond, it took Slater's eyes a few seconds to fully size up the fact that he was not alone in the hut.

Behind the desk, his face composed, his dark, bottomless eyes regarding Slater with a placid calm as he sat leaning back on a high leather chair, was a man familiar to Slater from photos he had scanned prior to the mission.

The man said a few words to one of the Shan regulars who had brought him inside, and a chair was pulled aside, then he was shoved into it.

After another crisp order Slater heard the door of the hut close behind him.

He was now alone with the drug warlord Kuhn Sa.

26

Strike day three.

Superior jungle craft and renewed confidence in their mission worked in favor of Hawke and Bishop, heightening their morale and investing them with renewed energy and a bolstered sense of purpose.

By the early-morning hours of strike day three, they had avoided detection by a second patrol of Shan United regulars and had come within recon distance of Kuhn Sa's mountain power base.

During the down time during which they had hidden from the paramilitary ground troops pursuing them, Hawke and Bishop had evolved a probe strategy that they hoped would enable them to recon the main base without detection.

The probe phase of the assault-rescue mission would be conducted in two discrete stages. The first stage would be soft and peripheral. The second, hard and deep.

First the two-man team would surveil the base from positions of low observability to the enemy. When they had collected sufficient Intelligence data to commence preparation for the strike into the base itself, the second, or assault, phase would then be initiated.

It was not now feasible, however, to make use of the AN/PRC radio units for purposes of tactical coordination and communication as preparations for the strike intensified or, for that matter, during the penetration and interdiction phase of the mission itself.

While the radios functioned normally, there was no means of ascertaining that Slater's commo unit had not fallen into enemy hands and thus that the team's communications link would remain uncompromised during the course of the mission.

Hawke and Bishop would communicate by other, more primitive methods, methods perfected by American servicemen in the bush of jungle hard zones from Bataan to the Iron Triangle.

Simulated bird calls and trail blazes would serve as reasonably secure communications channels in lieu of sophisticated electronic means, and these crude methods would get the job done.

Having dug their initial hole in a jungle hillside that allowed them a clear vantage point onto the base compound, Hawke and Bishop commenced their surveillance probe phase.

They began collecting usable Intelligence almost immediately as they took note of troop movements in and out of, around and through, Kuhn Sa's Shan Mountain strongbase.

As elapsed mission time counted down to zero, their covert surveillance began to yield a wealth of useful tactical data to the pair of SLAM strikers watching the base from the concealment of the jungle bush.

Surveillance yielded the data, for example, that perimeter patrols were carried out in a haphazard, unstructured manner, the sentries pausing to exchange pleasantries and light up cigarettes as they walked the wire.

Another item of potential significance to Bishop and Hawke that came to light during the soft-probe phase was that the Shan United forces had made no serious provisions against attack. None of the expected hardening of the facility's vulnerable points was in evidence.

Where military prudence might dictate berms or earthworks designed to hamper the progress of vehicles, there was only open ground.

Where an experienced soldier would emplace revetments protecting triple-A batteries from ground assault, there were only a few haphazardly sited machine-gun pits, none of them manned during the time SLAM's surveillance phase ran its course.

But the capstone of the Intelligence data gathered by Hawke and Bishop was their eyewitness sighting of Deal Slater as he was brought out of the prison hut and force-marched across the parade ground to what must have been the commander's hut early in their watch.

The sighting, as well as other aspects of the tactical observations of Bishop and Hawke, was captured on fast film via a telephoto-lens-equipped Nikon for prestrike target analysis.

Seeing that Slater was still alive brought renewed hope to Hawke and Bishop.

Had operational circumstances not prevented it, they would both have done dances worthy of any football player at the close of a winning game.

Under the circumstances, they settled for slapping each other five.

A DARK RIVULET OF BLOOD flowed from the gash in Slater's scalp and ran into his eyes through the stained cloth that covered them.

He braced himself for the blow of the stick that came crashing down into his face again and nearly lost consciousness when the hardwood cudgel crashed against his skull.

Blindfolded, he couldn't see the face of the man who had been beating him, steadily and brutally and with a professional's precise skill, for the past several hours.

Slater recognized the voice of the questioner, though. It belonged to Kuhn Sa himself, who continued to barrage him with questions relative to the mission that had brought him to the Golden Triangle.

Kuhn Sa spoke in a calm, controlled voice, using precise if somewhat accented English, while his alter ego delivered punishment with a savage, unrelenting and machinelike intensity.

It was a combination of relentless brutality and tireless probing that Slater had no doubt had broken very quickly many others who had been subjected to it, perhaps even quicker than many of the much-touted but not much more effective truth drugs favored by the writers of spy novels.

In reality, continuous beatings augmented by unceasing questioning, often complemented by electrical shock to the genitals, had proved the time-tested means of extracting information from unwilling sources throughout the history of modern warfare.

It was apparent that Kuhn Sa and his unseen henchman were masters of this savage though useful art.

They pressed Slater unrelentingly, but they also took great care never to inflict injury serious enough to cause death.

He had known from the outset that his captors would take note of his wounded leg and he found he had anticipated correctly. Kuhn Sa's torturer had paid special attention to Slater's wound, striking it repeatedly during his ordeal.

Subjected to such grueling punishment, Slater had passed out at least twice during his interrogation, but was brought around by having water poured over his head before the beating and the interrogation proceeded again.

Now, after sustaining several hours of torture, Slater again braced himself for a renewed assault by the stick-wielding torturer whom he expected to strike him any second.

But the blow did not come.

A barked command from Kuhn Sa stayed the torturer's hand, and Slater heard the man's footsteps as he left the commander's hut then descended the porch steps leading to ground level.

"We will talk again, my stubborn friend," Kuhn Sa told Slater. His bloodstained blindfold was removed by Shan United regulars who had appeared in the torturer's place, and he was ushered from the commander's hut.

The sun had climbed to its zenith as Slater emerged from the hut and it stung his eyes, swollen from lack of sleep and the effects of the beating he had sustained.

In fact, his entire face had swollen up from the effects of the beating, and his leg, traumatized by repeated blows of the torturer's stick, was hurting far more than when he had received his wound initially.

Had he not been supported by the two Shan Army regulars who carried him across the compound, Slater would have had to crawl toward his hut.

When he reached it, one of them supported him while the other unlocked its door, and he was thrown inside. The paramilitaries left laughing as Slater pulled himself into a sitting position with his back up against one of the bamboo walls.

In a way he was thankful for the brutality shown him by the guards: for a fleeting instant Slater had felt a strange gratitude for their aid in his negotiating the compound, a feeling that he recognized as the first stage of a dangerous syndrome developed by captives.

Slater realized that this was only the first symptom of an eventual psychological change that could only be resisted to a finite point by anyone held in captivity.

Cracks had already appeared in his psyche, and it was through those fractures that Kuhn Sa would try to auger down into the depths of his mind, shattering his resolve and breaking him entirely.

It wouldn't happen, though. Before he was broken, Slater would either have escaped Kuhn Sa's power base or be dead.

There would not be any in-between.

27

A few hours past midnight of strike day four, Mason Hawke and Eddie Bishop were ready to carry out the second and final phase of their recon.

Soft probe would turn hard as steel and hot as fire.

Both men knew that the corridor for action was now open but would not remain that way indefinitely.

Slater was alive; this fact they had established conclusively. But they had watched as he had been led away, beaten and bloodied, barely able to walk, and the two combat veterans had no illusions about how long a man in such condition could hold out.

Even the best of men could not last for long, Slater's capabilities notwithstanding.

Prior to mobilizing for the blitz on the Shan base, Bishop and Hawke checked their weapons. The down time of surveillance had not been wasted. They had used part of the lull period to take down their Barret H-Bars in order to clean and oil every moving part of the advanced-design guns.

The .50-caliber machine guns were reloaded, as many metal surfaces as possible wrapped with electrical tape to minimize clatter.

In order to break up the telltale outlines of the barrel and receiver, these parts were covered with expandable camo-patterned webbing material to make the weapon profile fuzzy and minimize the risk of detection.

Similarly dressed were the Colt Commando XM177E2 assault weapons, which had been carried as auxiliary support armament on their rucksacks.

Among the weapons for which SLAM's training routine demanded proficiency, the Commando was a primary armament.

The Commando was not designed as a true assault rifle. The resemblance between the Commando and its close relative, the Colt M-16A2 Model 723, have in part fostered this widely held though inaccurate notion.

Where the 723 was standardly equipped with a short barrel and flash suppressor, the Commando's business end terminated in a heftier muzzle brake, necessary in order to stabilize the weapon during full-automatic fire.

Although classed as a submachine gun, the Commando nevertheless packs the full measure of firepower delivered by all members of the M-16 family. The Commandos ported by Hawke and Bishop were of a special breed, as well.

For one thing, they had been specially rifled by Colt technicians to the original one-in-fourteen twist that had enabled the early M-16 models to wreak such havoc on the enemy in Vietnam that the weapons had become the subject of peace talks in Geneva—a measure of firepower that had been deliberately curtailed in later versions of the famous rifle to produce terminal ballistics designed to wound rather than kill.

The second augmentation to the Commandos ported by the SLAM team was the modified Sionic-type sound suppressor threaded to the muzzle in compatibility with the standard muzzle-brake attachment.

The Sionics would not only enable the two SLAM team members to deliver whispering death to a ruthless enemy, but would also well serve to hide muzzle-flash and stabilize the weapon as well or better than production models of the gun.

While the Barrets would ride TEAM combat harnesses, the Commandos would come out of storage for deployment in the penetration phase of the mission.

These short-barreled weapons, too, were wrapped in flexi-netting to conceal their profiles prior to zero hour. With armament secure and weapons safed prior to commencement of the strike, Bishop and Hawke assisted one another in applying asymmetrical stripes of nonreflective camouflage paint to their faces.

Faces cammied up, hands protected by tactical gloves, their NVGs securely strapped to their heads, which were in turn covered by black Orlon watch caps, the two strikers advanced on their target with caution and stealth, annihilation and salvation their twin operational goals.

MINUTES LATER, Bishop and Hawke had penetrated the compound perimeter, dispensing swift termination to two sentries encountered during the initial seconds of their stealthy and lethal incursion.

A sound-suppressed Commando burst of 5.56 mm tumbling ammunition took the life of Hawke's man, striking him in the heart zone and tearing a ragged hunk out of his upper-left torso before dropping him to the ground, where a second quickly delivered burst stilled his final convulsions.

Bishop took his sentry from behind, using the steel end plate of the Commando's extended, scissor-type buttstock to deliver a crushing blow to the side of the sentry's head.

This pile-driving sidearm blow caved in his skull and instantly damaged critical motor centers in his brain. A burst of silenced automatic fire to the prone figure ensured that the sentry died quickly and, above all, quietly.

When both fresh kills were dragged to positions of concealment, the SLAM rescue element stood stock-still only several meters inside the perimeter of the base.

As they probed in glowing electronic space through their night vision goggles, they were aware that the broken pattern of light and dark of their combat dress, combined with their cammied faces, tactical-gloved hands and black watch caps, rendered them virtually invisible to any but close-in observers.

Establishing that there was an unobstructed corridor for stealthy movement toward the prison hut in which the rescue element anticipated finding Slater, Hawke and Bishop negotiated the shadowed compound with senses honed to the keenness of a razor's edge by experience, training and by the primitive high brought on by adrenaline coursing through their bloodstreams.

Before long they had reached the vicinity of the prison hut where Slater was being held captive.

Pausing briefly to permit a base sentry to pass on his walk of the wire and waiting until the steady cadence of his jungle boots had receded entirely from hearing, Hawke moved toward the padlocked door while Bishop scanned the area, his silenced weapon ported at the ready.

Not wanting to venture even so much as a whisper because he was well aware of the distance that even the faintest sounds can carry in the jungle stillness, Hawke unshipped the wire cutters that he had brought from his rucksack and immediately went to work on the lock.

It was off its hasp in seconds, and Hawke went inside.

He was immediately grasped from behind by a powerfully muscled forearm and spun half-around. Something sharp at the corner of Hawke's field of view was moving quickly toward the side of his head.

Before colliding with it, the object stopped short.

"Damn it, Hawke," said Deal Slater, who now faced him. "I nearly punched your ticket."

The object in his hand was a long, sharp sliver of bamboo that he had worked loose from one of the poles of which the wall was constructed. He had sat gathering his strength for hours, waiting until the deepest part of the night to make his move.

The sentries walked singly at night, the combat veteran had noted, and he had taken care to cultivate a rapport with one of these Shan Army regulars.

Slater had been almost ready to feign a plea for assistance aimed at this particular guard, intending to kill the man and commandeer his AKR autoweapon when suddenly he had heard the sounds of someone at the lock.

Deciding that whoever it was had come in order to move him somewhere at night and seeing only a single dim figure silhouetted outside the hut through chinks in the wall, Slater had decided to take his chances and make his attempt without delay, bargaining that if he was moved it would be to an even more secure facility.

"You would have deserved what you got for disobeying a direct order," Slater added to the commando. "You had no business coming after me."

"You can have me and Bishop court-martialed later," Hawke told his boss, handing him a Commando SMG and a couple of spare 5.56 mm magazines. "Right now we're getting you out of this hellhole. Can you walk?"

"Yeah, I think so," Slater replied. "But tomorrow you might have been too late. Kuhn Sa was not screwing around."

Checking the Commando's clip out of longtime habit and making sure the fire select was set on full auto, Slater also accepted minigrenades from Hawke.

Reclosing the door as silently as possible and replacing the sheared-off lock so at first glance it would appeared secured, Hawke and Slater joined Bishop for the extraction phase of the rescue operation.

28

Before the false dawn came, Hawke had unshipped the satcom-satellite-uplinked comm unit and was speaking with Convention via secure encrypted transmission.

Within a matter of minutes, the unconventional-warfare unit's technical officer had relayed the updated status and position of the SLAM strike team and had called in the air-support element of the covert strike operation.

SHORTLY THEREAFTER, the bat-winged F117A Stealth fighter-bomber aircraft was taxiing for take-off from its covert base in Riyadh, Saudi Arabia. Its mission was to conduct a second bomb strike in the clandestine theater of operations.

Even as the bat-shaped low-observable aircraft got airborne, the flight crew on board the Navy frigate *Fort Worth* was embarking on preparations of their own.

These preparations concerned readying the Pave Low chopper, which was presently warming up on board, for a covert flight into the rally point designated by Hawke during transmission in order to stage a heliborne extraction from the combat zone.

It would be another several hours yet before the Stealth fighter came within range to deliver its lethal munitions payload; however, SLAM had plenty of things to occupy itself with until that time.

Because of Slater's escape and the strike on Kuhn Sa's base itself, reprisals were bound to be launched as soon as the American commando's absence was discovered.

Soon the jungle would be alive with hunters, searching for their elusive quarry.

HAVING ANTICIPATED that the drug warlord would be stung by Slater's escape into ordering a full-court press to apprehend the commandos, the SLAM team crafted its plans accordingly.

The linchpin of the strike team's strategy continued to be the mission's original objective.

This was an interdiction strike on the main poppy field located in a mountain valley lying near the United Shan Army encampment where Slater had been held prisoner by Kuhn Sa. The strike was then and would now be intended to decimate a bumper harvest of the opium poppy before it could be brought in.

Due to the team's transmission to Convention, the F117A Stealth fighter tasked with putting the munitions payload in the strike basket had already been dispatched and was pulling sub-Mach numbers to reach its destination in time.

The laser-guided air-to-ground munitions package carried by the aircraft would not have a high probability of reaching its target from the F117A's high-altitude flight envelope without a target paint from in theater.

Without the target paint, the Paveway ordnance-delivery package would be partially blind. The munitions package, once pickled off, could then be a nonstarter.

On the ground, in theater, it would be Mason Hawke's vital mission role to facilitate a target paint for Paveway to lock on to and put the ordnance in the strike basket.

The job of Deal Slater and Eddie Bishop would be to play the Judas goat, leading Kuhn Sa's paramilitary army as far away from Hawke's vulnerable position on the ground for as long as possible.

Long enough for the F117A to reach its preplanned drop zone and jettison its munitions package.

AFTER CONDUCTING a recon of the terrain, Mason Hawke made for a point on the perimeter of the poppy field that would provide him with two vital options.

The first of these options was the presence of a wide viewing horizon.

The second option was a secure corridor of retreat once the countdown had reached zero and the F117A was in position overhead for the scheduled munitions drop.

Consulting his digital wrist chronometer, Hawke noted that the strike would commence within a brief matter of time.

He began setting up the LTID laser illumination beacon to paint the target with the invisible beam of coherent light that the Paveway's seeker head would zero in on with a high degree of accuracy and reliability.

Ahead of him, amid stands of high grass, Hawke could see the waving field of red poppies, each of them three to four feet high and most not yet fully open.

The field extended for some eighty meters to the encircling jungle tree line surrounding it. A musty odor that smelled something like a blend of turpentine and new-mown hay hung over the field.

Below each bright red flower nodding in the gentle breeze, set high on the stem, was a bulging egg-sized pod, greenish tan in color.

It was from this pod, nicked for its pungent sap, that the opium sap came from which heroin was derived, the most profitable result of a refining process that stretched from Asia to Europe and across the sea to American shores.

After initializing the LTID and allowing a brief warm-up period, Hawke squinted through the laser device's sighting reticle.

This showed him that the beam was focused on the approximate center of the poppy field, and the eyes-up digital readout display superimposed above the reticle viewscreen added data on range, elevation and azimuth, as well as the length of time the unit had been energized.

With the LTID now fully deployed in the field, Hawke switched on the satcom transceiver unit the strike team had used in order to communicate with its base.

Because Slater's AN/PRC comset had been taken by the Shan troopers and had not been recovered on his escape, the two surviving comsets were parceled out to Slater and Bishop on field maneuvers in the jungle while Hawke was to use the satcom in a three-way communications system with himself as the main tactical node.

Having energized the satcom unit, Hawke transmitted on the wavelength established by the team as their primary communications channel.

Implementation of voice transmissions was warranted by the fact that although Slater's AN/PRC set was presumed to be still in enemy hands, their existence in the field was already compromised.

"Diamond to Zircon," Hawke began, using Slater and Bishop's call sign. "Quarterback is imminent."

There was static on the line as Hawke waited for his partners' reply. After waiting a few seconds and rechecking his readouts to assure himself that he was in fact transmitting on the correct frequency, Hawke again transmitted the message.

"Good to go, Diamond," he heard Slater's voice in his earbud a few moments later.

In the background there was the sound of distant, rapid automatic fire, a sound that his ears, attuned to the racket, made out toward the east, over the jungle to one side.

"Taking fire and could not respond. Making for Cleaver now. Good hunting."

"Roger, Zircon," Hawke returned immediately, "and the same. Will RV at Cleaver on commencement of Quarterback. Out."

Hawke retracted the satcom's antenna and stowed the unit back in his pack, which lay on the ground beside him as he crouched behind the LTID.

In the warm stillness of the jungle, punctuated now only by the buzzing of insects and the occasional sounds from the treetops made by monkeys and birds, Hawke could clearly hear the steady pulse of a new spasm of automatic-weapons fire.

29

Slater and Bishop had been playing a deadly game of tag with the Shan United Army troopers who were beating the bush to hunt them down.

Staying agile, mobile and hostile, the SLAM commandos shadowed the flanks and rear of the hunters' formations, whittling down their numbers and spreading confusion and anger through the ranks by staging highly damaging and highly mobile sniper attacks.

Followed by rapid movements from their positions, the commandos were far from the shooting ground by the time the enemy reached their positions.

By then they had already deployed to new positions where the much-harried enemy did not suspect their presence, waiting for the right moment to strike again.

These tactics were in service of a strategy aimed not only in breaking the cohesion of the enemy force but also in accomplishing something else: herding the Shan United troops as far away from Hawke's position as possible in order to maximize the chances for a successful hit by the munitions payload to be dropped by the F117A.

Now again, after striking the enemy, Slater and Bishop took up positions at an angle to the main element of the body of Shan troopers. Roughly at company strength, this infantry patrol was moving up the shallow slope of a jungle-covered ridge.

Taking up the specially silenced and enhanced Colt Commando SMGs, which were now studded on select-fire modes, Slater and Bishop each picked their targets and squeezed off precisely targeted single rounds of tumbling 5.56 mm ammunition.

The result of these actions was as destabilizing to the enemy forces as it was predictable to the SLAM detachment.

Slater and Bishop had seen those same effects repeated time and time again in the course of using the hit-and-git tactics against their highly motivated though heavy-handed pursuers.

After each trigger squeeze of the Commandos, a Shan trooper suddenly dropped to the ground, ready for the undertaker.

There was no telltale crack of gunfire or muzzle-flash to give away the position of the shooters. There was not even any overt indication that a bullet had been the means responsible for causing death.

No sound, no flash.

Nothing to give the game away.

All that the opposition perceived was that one of their number was suddenly dying before their eyes without any discernible cause and—they had learned after their attempts to find and kill the unseen enemy—with no retaliatory action possible.

Slater and Bishop saw the enemy force break apart into a confused jumble of frightened, hot-tempered men whose identity as infantry soldiers had been chipped away by the successive strikes to expose the untrained rabble just beneath.

Using the jungle terrain for cover as the combination of field craft, camo paint and camouflage fatigues made the SLAM strikers virtually invisible, Slater and Bishop took notice of the havoc that their strategy had caused.

Their pursuers now cast about in vain for the source of the destruction to which they had been exposed but came up empty.

By now the two SLAM strikers had succeeded not only in decimating their foes but also in reducing their effectiveness by a significant margin.

The Shan United paramilitary troops were miserable, and their morale was low. But in addition to these accomplishments, Slater and Bishop had almost herded their hunters into the kill box they had prepared for them.

With the F117A munitions drop imminent, the next phase of the action would be to deploy toward the rally point code-named Cleaver.

Once at Cleaver, the unconventional-warfare specialists would link up with Hawke and await the arrival of the armored Pave Low helicopter gunship that had been sent to get them out of the mission zone.

Selecting a suitable spot for the deployment of a claymore mine kill trap, Slater and Bishop deployed the claymores in a phased array for a three-way break.

Supplemented by automatic fire from the Commandos, conditions were good to facilitate a high mortality rate among the unfriendlies caught in the trap.

After siting the claymores with their concave surfaces pointing toward the enemy's line of entry into the kill trap and the detonation wires deployed to a small fire-control panel whose buttons would allow Slater to detonate the claymores in a series of lethal pulses, Bishop left Slater on the high ground perpendicular to one edge of the trap. Bishop then redeployed to an area situated at the head of the zone laced with the remote-triggered antipersonnel land mines.

"Go!" he heard Slater's voice in his comset earbud as the Shan United troops finally came into position.

At this notification of imminent meltdown, Bishop opened up with the Commando now on burst-fire mode and with the sound suppressor unthreaded.

The disorientated force of soldiers, now hearing the sound of ratcheting autofire and seeing muzzle-flash in the distance where there had been none before, immediately rushed pell-mell toward the source of the gunfire without thinking that they were being led into a trap.

Soon the force was in the kill trap.

Waiting a few beats, Slater triggered the phased claymores.

The first claymore exploded, killing several enemy troops at the head of the column and setting off the expected chain reaction, which corralled the rest of the trapped Shan regulars back toward the rear of the column. There they were met with shrapnel and blast from the other claymores down the line exploding right behind the first antipersonnel munitions charge.

While this carnage was taking place, Slater and Bishop were saturating the killing zone from above with 5.56 mm automatic-weapons fire.

In a matter of seconds the violent spasm of destruction unleashed by the claymores and the autofire had taken out the entire force of Shan United infantry pursuers.

Breaking from their positions, Slater and Bishop proceeded quickly through the jungle on a preplanned path to rally point Cleaver. They knew that the munitions drop would commence within a matter of minutes.

They needed to be ready and in position within seconds after it went down.

MASON HAWKE CONSULTED his wrist chronometer and took note of the fact that in a matter of minutes the field of poppies wafting in the gentle breeze would be turned into a fireball of near-total destruction.

Well away from the Quarterback strike zone, Hawke would be in little danger from the blast and would not leave the area until he had a visual confirm on the success of the drop.

It was a testament to the accuracy of precision-guided conventional munitions that such a thing was possible. If not for the Paveway guidance enhancement upgrade to the dumb iron bomb to be deployed by the F117A, Hawke might as well have been sitting on the center of a bull's-eye.

Hawke checked the LTID's sighting reticle again as the final minutes to zero-hour ticked off. It was immediately after taking his eyes from the scope that Hawke suddenly spotted a squad of soldiers where none should have been.

The Shan United infantry troops came walking out of the thicket at the jungle tree line and cut directly across the poppy field. To his chagrin, Hawke realized that the O.D.-garbed paramilitaries were staring right down the bore sight of the laser and could not help but detect the glowing light of its emitter.

In a moment the squad was moving toward his position, their weapons cocked and unsafed.

With seconds before the drop commenced, Hawke cranked up the bipodded Barret MG and opened fire on the troops in the poppy field, forcing the squad of foot soldiers to tuck their heads down.

Having given away his position by launching his assault, Hawke's option was to continue to pour suppressing fire down on the Shan regulars pinned down in the field until the F117A munitions drop commenced.

Soon, though, more troops came pouring out of the jungle tree line at an angle from the first group, cutting diagonally across the field toward his emplacement. As they entered the field of waist-high poppies, the men dropped down and commenced to fire their AK weapons at Hawke, who answered with .50-caliber machine-gun fire.

The contest that had pitted raw numbers against a well-sited machine-gun emplacement with better range and heavier firepower resulted in a stalemate that ended when, from an altitude of fifty thousand feet, the F117A dropped its payload.

Hawke had just opened up with the Barret to lay down a stream of fire on the second wave of advancing Shan troops. Seconds later the iron bomb containing the napalm and chemical defoliant mixture, homing in on the dot of laser light by means of the Paveway's seeker head, exploded in a concentrated burst.

The results of the Quarterback air strike were as instantaneous as they were devastating.

Where there had been a field of gaudy red flowers and troops firing guns only seconds before, there was now a rapidly spreading sunburst of incandescent flame, rising with the roar of a thunder that drowned out the screams of men dying within the center of the firestorm.

Hawke had his confirm.

He quickly stowed the LTID laser-targeting illumination unit and moved out of the area with rally point Cleaver as his objective.

30

Slater and Bishop were suddenly taking fire.

Navigating the jungle landscape, they had come within a few-score meters of the clearing that was the rally point for the Pave Low helicopter extraction.

There they were surprised by an unexpected concentration of Shan United troops of at least company strength.

With the jungle foliage sparser now as they gained the high elevations of the mountains, concealment could not be depended on as much by the SLAM commandos.

This meant that part of their tactical edge was given away to the opposition, which also had a vast numerical superiority over their quarry going in their favor.

The result was a firefight that neither Slater nor Bishop had wanted to get into, but circumstances forced them to accept it just the same.

With the enemy targeting on them, Slater sent back answering salvos from his Commando 5.56 mm autoweapon while Bishop used the Barret heavy machine gun to launch .50-caliber tracers into the center of the company.

The combination of heavy firepower subjected the attacking force to a punishingly high casualty rate, teaching them a newfound caution and forcing them to tuck their heads down. For the time being they were effectively suppressed by the skillfully vectored small-arms fire.

Slater and Bishop used the fleeting lull that their counterattack had bought them to break from cover and stage a fighting retreat toward the rally point.

Seconds after their mobilizing, pulses of heavy-caliber fire from the enemy's chattering autorifles were walking toward them across the jungle terrain as they pushed ahead toward the rally point.

They reached the RV with a slim lead on the advancing enemy troops and immediately took up defensive positions behind the cover of fallen trees while the enemy pressed on their position.

As they fired at the advancing phalanx of Shan United troops in their jungle O.D.s, who were coming in despite taking heavy fire, there was still no sign of Hawke.

And then, above the thunderous din raised by the bolt clatter of their fast-cycling automatic weapons, Slater and Bishop realized that the sound of another Barret heavy-barreled machine gun had been added to the reports of their own guns.

It was Bishop who first spotted Hawke hunkered at the edge of the clearing at about a sixty-degree angle to their own position.

He was firing from a crouch, and the pulses of flame bratting from the barrel of his weapon, the .50-caliber squad auto, highlighted his position on the perimeter of the clearing.

Catching sight of their partner gave the two embattled covert strikers renewed confidence as Bishop and Slater continued to pour fire at the shooters in the bush.

Aware that they would be unable to hold out for much longer against the overwhelming firepower and troop strength of the unfriendlies, who appeared oblivious to their high casualty count, the SLAM commandos continued to lean on the triggers of their guns.

Their ammo reserves were running dangerously low when the beleaguered warriors heard the telltale sound of the Pave Low as the enormous gunship circled near the extraction zone.

Slater immediately put down his weapon and unshipped two red smoke grenades to mark the extraction site for the Pave Low's crew.

Infrared strobes had been originally intended for their scheduled night pickup, but popping smoke in the conventional manner was now the way to go.

Tossing the canister charges into the center of the clearing, Slater again took up his Commando SMG and started shooting as twin plumes of dense red smoke started to rise above the clearing and, taken by the brisk wind, were wafted up toward the tops of the tall trees encircling it.

Slater and Bishop signaled across the clearing to Hawke, communicating that he was to cover their retreat toward the chopper and then move himself.

The enemy, too, had seen the Pave Low chopper and knew that their hated opponents were about to elude their grasp unless they somehow found a way to stop them cold.

Immediately they increased the pace and tempo of their fire, intent on bringing down the interlopers before they could slip right through their fingers.

The Pave Low's door gunners also opened up on the enemy, the glowing 7.62 mm tracers of the Miniguns merging into a rotoring awl of obliterating firepower as it punched its way through the trees and sought out the troops strung out along the jungle's edge.

The big combat chopper had now settled well below the tree line, hovering only a few feet above the grassy floor of the jungle clearing.

Slater and Bishop were already breaking from cover, firing as they sprinted on a low, hard-to-hit crouch toward the open rear hatchway, which promised safety from the spinning centrifuge of death in whose mad nucleus they had been trapped.

As they neared the side of the Pave Low, Hawke was up from his position several meters down the line from his two partners' fire station.

He had a greater distance to cover and, if not for the suppressing fire delivered by the Pave Low's door gunners and their fast-cycling Miniguns, his chances of making it to the chopper would have been marginal at best.

"Go! *Go!*" Slater and Bishop yelled above the chattering of their guns as they watched Hawke charge toward them through the hail of pummeling autofire.

Both men were chagrined when, midway across the clearing, Hawke suddenly seemed to trip over his feet and topple to the side.

Slater and Bishop saw that their partner was still alive as he tried to gain his feet, but he promptly fell over again.

Blood was gushing out of his left leg, apparently hit by the heavy enemy fire. At almost the same moment, the door gunner behind the Minigun was flung aside by a burst of 7.62 mm rounds, blood pumping from a hideous wound in his throat.

"Cover me!" Slater shouted, and before anyone could act he was already out the open hatch of the gunship, sprinting toward his partner who lay sprawling on the ground.

Bishop, reacting quickly, stepped behind the pistol-grip triggers of the now silent Minigun and began to fire into the tree line, covering Slater's sprint toward Hawke. Other members of the crew hefted automatic rifles and added their own salvos to the starboard Minigun, the only one, due to the chopper's position, that could be trained on the enemy.

Snapping off bursts from his Commando as he ran through the clearing, Slater soon reached Hawke's position. Supported by Slater, Hawke was able to half run, half hop toward the waiting chopper while both of them snapped off wild bursts at the enemy gathered just beyond the clearing's edge.

In a matter of seconds Slater was pushing Hawke into the grasping hands of the chopper's crew and had jumped in himself, while Bishop kept up the barrage from behind the Minigun.

"Go! Go! *Go!*" those in back yelled at the pilot, who immediately pushed forward on the cyclic and eased up the collective to deliver torque to the whirling rotors.

As heavy as it was, the Pave Low's powerful engines fed the big main rotors the torque they needed and the helicopter gunship shot straight up like a great steel-hulled phoenix ascending toward the sky.

All the while it was taking heavy fire from the Shan United troopers who had deployed into the clearing despite the withering fire laid down from both Miniguns as the chopper ascended.

But the titanium-armored hull of the Pave Low and the extra protection around its critical housings of components, such as its engines and fuel tanks, resisted the heavy fire from the ground forces below, while Slater and Hawke added the punch of the torching Barrets to the thunder of the Miniguns.

Within a matter of minutes, the Pave Low's steady rate of climb brought them out of range of the enemy's chattering guns.

Vectoring the helicopter to the south, the pilot followed the black line for home base as those on board who were capable tended to the wounded and the dead. Among those who would make it was Mason Hawke, who held up his thumb to Slater and Bishop as the crewman who served as medic bandaged his wounded leg.

"Good to go," he said.

EPILOGUE

Kuhn Sa walked from the barren field in which the scents of charred rock, blasted earth and fire-scorched vegetation mingled with the far fouler odors of recently burnt human flesh.

Surveying the scene, the drug warlord remained silent, his countenance etched with grave lines, as he moved back along the trail to his jungle encampment.

Those of his lieutenants who clustered around their leader noted the grim cast of his features and held their tongues. Fearful for their lives, they held back from volunteering any remarks, knowing that anything they said might not sit well with Kuhn Sa.

They had all lost friends and comrades during the covert strikes, and now, thanks to the interdiction of the enemy commandos who had come and gone with impunity, faced an uncertain future.

There would almost certainly be renewed strikes, probably from the Thais, as well, who would become emboldened by the success of the covert missions. It would be the hill people, deprived of the revenue of their harvest, who would suffer the most.

Cognizant of these facts, Kuhn Sa also realized that those around him were thinking about ways to replace him, but he also knew that none of them had the guts to make an assassination attempt.

For the present he had nothing to fear.

The poppy had been grown in these mountain valleys for thousands of years. It would be grown for hundreds, if not thousands more.

The insatiable demand of the Americans, and more recently, the Europeans, for the drug made from the poppies would not go unfilled. And although this field accounted for almost two-thirds of the season's crop, there were still other fields where the crop yield was intact.

Kuhn Sa knew that despite the severe blows he had been dealt, he would survive and live to gather up another harvest of the poppies.

His vast holdings in international accounts would provide a buffer between the wrath of the hill people and his own personal safety. Their bellies filled, their anger would soon dissipate.

Most of all, Kuhn Sa knew that the political resolve of the Americans would change in time.

Administrations came and went, and public opinion had a great impact on the distant nation's will and ability to act. In wreaking destruction on the massive scale they had, the Americans had miscalculated.

Ironically their very actions had planted the seeds of their undoing amid the charred wasteland that had formerly been a field of poppies. Kuhn Sa turned back to see the men with video cameras wrap up their taping of the charred corpses littering the napalmed field.

Before long the American media would find themselves in possession of copies of that tape, and the inescapable parallels with Vietnam would be drawn.

Kuhn Sa's cunning mind had already begun to move forward in time, to the moment when the first requests would come from Western camera crews to come into this territory and film the carnage.

Yes, he knew.

He would triumph in the end.

As the inspection tour neared the drug warlord's encampment, the mood of his retainers had also lightened; for the first time in many days, they had seen the flicker of a smile play across Kuhn Sa's face.

Communism's death throes bring the
world to the edge of doom in

DON PENDLETON'S

THE EXECUTIONER®

FEATURING

MACK BOLAN®

BATTLE
FORCE

The dynamic conclusion to the FREEDOM TRILOGY finds Mack
Bolan, Able Team and Phoenix Force battling to avert World
War III. From the war-torn states of Eastern Europe to the urban
hellgrounds of Los Angeles, Bolan's army fights to head off a
nightmare of chemical warfare.

Take
4 explosive books
plus a
mystery bonus
FREE

Past and future collide with deadly
force in the Middle East in

David Alexander's

NOMAD

D E S E R T   F I R E

**With his commando fighting skills and superior covert-
operations tactics, Nomad is a lethal weapon against
techno-terrorism's continued bid for power.**

**A brilliant research scientist turned psychotic guru
searches for power linked to hidden ancient energy
spheres, located somewhere in the Middle East. Nomad
stalks his quarry through space and time—final
destination, Iraq 1991, where this madman will join
forces with a powermonger whose evil vision will
unleash an orgy of death and destruction.**

Step into the future with the second installment of

JAKE STRAIT

BOGEYMAN

by FRANK RICH

In Book 2: **THE DEVIL KNOCKS,** Jake Strait is the chosen hero of the hour as he tries to take control of an impregnable fortress called Denver.

Jake Strait is a licensed enforcer in a future world gone mad—a world where suburbs are guarded and farmlands are garrisoned around a city of evil.